BECAUSE WITCHES ARE ALWAYS WOMEN

MAP OF THE HINTERLANDS OF HORI & THEREABOUTS

For Djiah

RICHA LAKHERA is an award-winning TV journalist and author of six novels. Her diverse experience in storytelling and communications has taken shape in various platforms. Her novels encompass myriad cultural sub-sets in multiple genres, including crime thrillers, revenge dramas, supernatural adventure and young adult coming-of-age stories. Four of her English novels have been translated into Hindi and several titles have been picked up for film adaptation and OTT. Her books are available on AUDIBLE.

Richa has worked as deputy editor and senior correspondent at NDTV 24x7 and NDTV India for over a decade. She is the recipient of Excellence in Entertainment Journalism Award 2016 from the Indian Council for UN Relations (ICUNR) and the recipient of 1000 Women of Excellence in Asia, Womennovator Awards 2021. She completed her master's in chemistry from Miranda House (DU).

Trained in the fine arts, Richa has conceptualised the online art gallery, Bombay Coral, which can be viewed at https://richalakhera.in/

Also by Richa Lakhera:

History of Violence (forthcoming)
Hungry Gods
Garbage Beat
Item Girl

Contamination

Richa Lakhera

Om Books International

First published in 2022 by

Om Books International

Corporate & Editorial Office
A-12, Sector 64, Noida 201 301
Uttar Pradesh, India
Phone: +91 120 477 4100
Email: editorial@ombooks.com
Website: www.ombooksinternational.com

Sales Office
107, Ansari Road, Darya Ganj,
New Delhi 110 002, India
Phone: +91 11 4000 9000
Fax: +91 11 2327 8091
Email: sales@ombooks.com
Website: www.ombooks.com

ISBN: 978-93-92834-72-1

Printed in India

10 9 8 7 6 5 4 3 2 1

BEFORE

The little girl searched long for her mother. Near the sacred boundaries of the Jotsoma forest, where they used to roam at will, she halted. Her mother hung from the old oak tree, a stalactite of flesh growing towards the earth. Trussed up with a rope around her neck, she swayed gently in the wind, an ornament of death, shining pale through the light of the bright moon.

But she was not dead yet. Eyes fluttering open, the dying woman's gaze rested on her daughter. Softly she sighed, her final breath weaving a strange language in the air about them. When she became still, the curious pendant on her neck crumpled to the ground. The girl clasped it to her heart, hissing curses at the mob who came for her next.

It happened then. Sheaths of fog swiftly materialised into a dripping mist so dense that all became invisible to one another at a distance of half a dozen yards, and even the country was blotted from sight. By the time the mist dispersed, the girl had vanished. Left behind was a rancid smell, a fetid heat, and hoofprints in the stone, as if it were the softest wax.

Some still hear the girl wailing as seasons change, accompanied by the howls of beasts. Since then, even the strongest dare not enter the Jotsoma after sunset.

⌘ US ⌘

The first madness was that She was born. That the gods stuffed Her into a bag of tiny human skin. The second madness was, the gods stuffed Her inside—with Us.

We came from somewhere, like everything else. Singled out, We were thrust into the birthing waters of Her mother, and into the small sleeping body forming within. Certain times, as now, We went by volition.

Once part of the bloodstream, We lost all volition and got locked into the blurred consciousness of the little mind—Hers. Trapped by the unfamiliar birthing of Her human body, which was also becoming—Ours.

We got used to the systematic warm thuds of the two heartbeats separated by flesh and blood and bone, since We were already used to the option of leaving and returning to the place We came from.

In the early months, when We tried to chat with Her, She, still forming, would kick up a storm in the womb. Still fresh from the other side, in the womb She spoke to Us in the special language. But all that would change the moment She was thrust outside into the human world.

1

The search patrol walked in blood frozen solid. The cold was a knife pressed permanently to the cheek, a constant reminder that the bleak lands of Hori were first inhabited by the tribes who had to eat each other to stay alive in winter. The season had been uncharacteristically long and dark and there was something mythical about its slow progression from snow to thaw to snow again, to mud and misery to sickness, as if, in living through it, they were passing through many ages.

The hunt for the missing *Habishi* villagers was now reaching the hills buried in mist. Eyes fogged with white breath from their mouths, the mountain Resistance Militia patrol, led by Amba, trudged in grim silence. They had walked every single bridge and treaded in knee-deep slush and followed muddy streams and searched every single track, and as the second day drew to an end, the search for the lost men was advanced into the remote stretch of the Hori mountains; the perfect setting for fear-spurred nightmares coming to life, if one wasn't careful enough.

The battle-hardened squad was not yet calling Amba a death-wish behind her back. First gunner Gora, a favourite of hers, was still alive, still dreaming of tender chicken fried in maguey oil and in layers of unblemished bread and expensive rice. Her best men, Solon, Rodh and Kunta, had not yet hurt an eye or lost a limb to the blood-lust of mad Colonel Madbull's murderous army, the Red-Hounds, who had only one agenda—to exterminate each and every member of the Resistance Militia. The rest of the men who would be injured were still perfectly healthy, and the others, who would die, were still perfectly alive and optimistic after a week of inflicting substantial damages on the Red-Hounds, not just by barrel, but by planting explosives. Retaliation stalked them, deadlier than their wildest dreams, but they did not know that yet. Amba's own dreams had not become as bad yet; at least the ones she would remember.

The lookout continued till dawn, when, at last, the group came close upon the part where the villagers were last seen. The rear guard pressed closer, glancing nervously at the strange gaps in the rocks, for this was also the stretch where they expected to be attacked by wild animals. Amba tried to ignore the sensation of being surrounded by dead faces, set in hideous grimaces, floating along with them. Lama, the newest member, who had a habit of starting at the least sound, became the butt of jokes when, frightened of his own shadow, he seemed ready to dash away in mad flight. Tales of monster bats nesting in the Jotsoma hills, who flew from place to place in great swarms after sunset so large and bloodthirsty that they were rumoured to kill a horse, and even grown men, were taken seriously in their village.

Cutting a wide arc, Amba's torch threw a strong white light over the new territory. The suspension bridge, an old, rough-hewn contraption of crude wooden uprights, overlooked a deep crack on the earth's surface. Slick and alive with moss and undergrowth in various stages of decay, the crossbeams on the floor trembled at every step. All around, steep sides of the precipitous gorge were marred by deep gulches, cut jaggedly by dried torrents and ending in a confined subterranean ocean of rocks.

The wind picked up and struck Amba across the face. It rushed into her throat, battering its way into her belly as if all the sky was being funnelled through her, and though she gagged at its coldness and the way its swelling force poured on and on, choking off her breath, she pressed on, her will blazed up, stubborn and resistant.

Something like hair brushed against her feet. She swiped at it with her right hand and gagged and stepped back from the grinning corpse with a start. The way forward was blocked by a heap of dead bodies, a sight which froze her blood and filled her with pity and horror. Seemed like some spiteful animals had clawed out their vital organs. Around them, grinning like a dozen ravenous monsters filled with teeth, was certain death—grenades packed with nuts and bolts. Not expected to necessarily bring down structures, but rip open, kill all soft skin targets, which meant animals and humans.

Amba held her hand up and motioned the squad to stop.

"God help us!" exclaimed Solon.

"We have to leave them. We have to go back," appealed Kunta, his legs ready to dodge any quick-flung missile.

"None of our own will be left for animals to feast on. Even if they are dead." Amba interrupted with that calm despair, which occurs only in a heart with strings of steel that yields to no danger.

"The dead are dead—won't feel anything, will they?" said Rodh.

"Their families would," she replied. "Will you help me pile them up?"

Rodh nodded strangely. It could just as well signify yes as no. In truth, terror sluiced through him at the thought of touching the grenades.

"Pile them up...?" he whispered.

"I will bury them. You pile up." She repeated in a low tone. Rodh came to his senses and there was a flush of colour on his mahogany face that said, *Don't look at me!*

"You have a better idea? They will *have* to be picked up." Amba spoke as though it was a matter of little consequence that they could be live grenades.

"Anyone?" She looked around and caught Solon's eye.

"By hand? That is suicide." Solon's eyes bulged. There was a singular absence of courage and heroic poses all around.

"You have a better plan?" asked Amba, if only to shut him up. As usual, Solon contributed little in a sticky situation.

"Alright. You pile them up. I reduce," said Kunta, but with deep reluctance.

"Good. Trust me," she said with a grateful nod towards Kunta. They waited for the rest of the squad to get into a safe perimeter.

The air was ripe with the scent of some revelation at hand. But, then, there always had been a necromantic vein buried in the *Habishis*, the ancient tribe to which they belonged. It was a strange undercurrent of emotion that concerned itself with a deep sense of not just blood or belonging, but also with mysticism and the downright inexplicable.

Amba seemed almost to be in a feral state as she bent down to pick up the crude grenades, shoulder muscles hard as stone, touch light as feather. Another wire. Infinite caution. Scratch of a nail. Another thump. And another. A ritual burn, a ceremony of the strange. Baffling. Though none of them had seen anything like that before, no one asked why and how she did it, perhaps not to jinx getting out alive. She scratched out little holes in the ground for the grenades and used a hand signal each time she put one there. Legs curled, elbows raised, her fingers deftly cutting the air. She seemed to have slipped from their world entirely and moved into another wild world from which humans had been erased. Her fingertips, her nose, her eyes, all seemed to possess a special intuition, an uncanny instinct which was never wrong. The weight, the texture of each grenade told a story, so did the smell, and her mind soaked in information with astonishing speed. Crystal clear senses, fully alert to the slightest of discrepancies in balance and composition. She frowned and tilted her head and held it with cautious concentration, as if it were a pitcher full of some caustic agent.

Three more. *Two* more. *One* more…

"We should get out of here."

Amba put the last grenade in the hole and stood with two fists held over her head. It seemed a conjuring trick, an almost alien perspective, something akin to madness.

"This place could be wired…never know, chlorine-mixed or daisy-chained."

Handling grenades is always the trickiest. Almost anything can explode anytime. One does not get time to break it down to *a b c*, separate the power source from the trigger, the trigger from the charge. Amba's skills could not be explained by any book because they were not derived from a manual. Eyes shining as telescopic sights of a sniper rifle, she pointed to a nearly invisible foam piece with the wire. It was daisy-chained to the penetrator variant of the regular grenades, which made entry points in the target it hit before exploding inside. The men froze. They could not believe their good luck that it did not blow up in their faces.

Danger gone, a great sunlight of relief seemed to drench them and everything was a second chance.

"The gods are with us." Solon was touching the wire under the foam.

"Wait, Solon, *no—ooo—stop—*"

Braaaaaaaaakkkkkkkkkkkkkkk!!!

Solon was about ten feet in the air, twisting and coming apart. His rifle and boots spun away as the shrapnel thudded into the shattered corpse, the force of it jerking limbs this way and that. The rest of them were knocked flat on their backs. Rodh lay in a corner, his helmet cracked against the pavement. His eyes were sheened with disbelief at what remained of his best friend. The air turned syrupy slow, flecked with dust and fear.

Solon had forgotten about the secondaries. One should never forget about the secondaries. Gora turned and stumbled out hastily, deathly sick, reeling over the bridge, and went shuddering up the horrible dim path beyond, clutching at the air for support, leaving the rest with exploding eardrums, jittery, some angry and some in tears, but grateful to be alive, to feel the pain. An angry mess of flesh and bones bore an awful remembrance that death occupied more area than the living. Plastic and rubber, burning somewhere in the background, in part killed the stench of burning flesh and blood. Faces puckered into grimaces from the smell of fresh blood as they finished scraping together Solon's pieces and scooped them all in bags. Even after the explosion faded away, the disturbed night was no longer dark and the road was covered with gusts of sparks and smoke.

Amba glanced across at Rodh. He averted his gaze. The few times their eyes met, a slow, dull resentment seeped out of him like coal gas, thin and sour. At that moment, there was something different externally about Amba, and all the men looked awkward beside her. In reality, a qualitative change had already set in, that was apparent to her.

One of the new recruits trembled when her sleeve brushed against his. It was the great chain of fear. The accusation, which they would not dare mouth aloud. The word. The miserable, degrading slur. They whispered with no regard, wrapped in a dreadful smirk and a fearful gaze—*Witch.*

⌘ HER ⌘

"Let her die," were the first words uttered when She was born. We know because We were there. They would soon start calling Her worse things. Her mother's thin body was prone to quick labour. The boy, the first child, was born in an hour. A crystal-eyed baby boy. The midwife got a fat fees when he came. He was given the name Nakul, the beautiful one.

She was still there in Her mother's womb. We were already anchored inside Her, asleep inside Her membranes, getting synced with Her mind, which was still forming.

She held against the pull for a week and a half before struggling into the world, slick and louder than a village of storms.

No one expected the frail, underweight infant to survive. She proceeded to die for several laborious hours, colour veering from dull grey to black and back to flesh. They had no idea about Her strength. The impatient midwife stopped Mother from feeding Her. Said it was a waste of good nursing milk. Neighbours advised Mother to feed the healthy boy instead. Pointing at Her crumpled head and arms and legs, the village doctor said there was a deformity.

Mother was adamant to not to let Her go without a fight. She shook Her violently, and when that failed, and as a last resort, put a finger in Her mouth, shook Her upside down and swaddled Her, and Us, close to her chest.

Newly born, She finally took a blazing breath. There was shock and amazement, mostly shock, at the tiny deformity kicking and squirming, pinned by the weight of Her weirdly shaped head. The notable thing about the birth was that She was born with a caul—a sign to the humans—She was set to be apart. The membrane covered two-thirds of Her head and face. Whoever wore the caul, humans believed, would never be lost in a forest, never drown in water, need not fear fire, and could not be poisoned. The midwife was fascinated, having never seen a caul. She would have succeeded in stealing it, had it not been for the watchful Mother who caught her in the act.

What they did not know was She was also Us. She was a promise, a curse, blood and bones tying it all together—an oath. A promise, an oath, made when She was a free and floating wave. When put inside human flesh, the oath became an object matter. And, as with all matter, She would eventually have a purpose. And until She discovered the purpose, it was Our job to stay hidden.

The Village-Shaman was summoned. He sensed Us instantly. He sensed the igneous rock, which was also Us—the secretion of Us over the years We stayed and ate and expelled the waste—the igneous rock, which lay at the pit of the baby's stomach. Between the mucus lining and the muscle layer to weigh Us down, after all, what was a microscopic stone to a child.

"Why are you inside the infant?" The Village-Shaman asked, but in his wildest dreams he did not expect Us to reply.

"We don't hide in a tree or inside the river. We hide in the velveteen inside the walls of Her skin. Who would notice the fragments woven in?"

The Village-Shaman shivered in fear when he heard Us. He hid it well. Outwardly, he moaned and lied: "You will never raise this one. Pray the Loki takes her. Her flesh will sate him and he will bless you with another healthy boy. Too many children on earth already. No room for such ones! This one will be dull as a rock, have less wit than bare ground and her hair will be matted—"

"Do not say such horrible words about my baby! Why is it better for her to die and not your child, or yours, or yours?" Mother wailed. "Look at the leaf—it got no sun, no soil, no rain, nothing; it grows out of stale wood, sour dust and feeds on stale water, which seeps into the rotten wood, yet, it survives and so shall my baby."

The Village-Shaman got a symbol, a dark circle of velvet black, a portable third eye, and affixed it to the baby's forehead, a smooth expanse of brand new skin. A sun to repel the evil eye, he said, to thwart the evil people who could coo at a child and curse it under their breath. We were curious. We wondered if it would work on Us.

"Patala has her eye on her. No good will come." The Village-Shaman wrung his hands.

"Old man, how dare you take the cursed name! The witch needs a doorway and you give that to her! You dare take the wretched name in the presence of my new born!"

"You can spit on me if I am wrong. It is your own fault if you come to grief. I will not lose sleep over this anymore."

The Village-Shaman refused to perform the birth ceremony, and without his sanction the child's name was considered impure. This maddened the Mother more than anything else. The pride. The mother screamed at the priest. He was adamant.

"Aren't you ashamed of yourself, woman?"

"Why should I be ashamed, Priest?"

"For parading that thing on the street!"

"It's a free country."

"Not for the likes of witches."

"Who says so?"

"Look at the little witch's eyes. How she stares!"

They chanted, led by the Village-Shaman. It was a signal for the others to start throwing whatever they could lay their hands on, at the mother. One of them picked up a sharp stone and aimed it at Her face. It missed Mother and hit Her on the head. It cut open Her baby skin. She did not cry out when Her skin leapt apart at the stone's sharp touch, though the pain must have been hot as a lightning strike.

Startled, She opened Her eyes on the outside world. And We looked out too. The attackers poised to throw their next bunch of stones, froze. They dropped them quietly and slunk back with fear. The skin cut open and bled red on Her smooth baby skin. Its abysmal roots already grew straight to Her heart. To Us.

She opened Her eyes inside too. She saw Us. She did not know who We were and what to do with Us. Neither did We. We were new to each other. It would take us time to get used to Her.

Mother gave Her a name: Amba.

As the years passed, She stopped talking to Us. Stopped taking Us seriously. Soon, She started ignoring Us. She thought of Us as some mental parasite with many heads. Perhaps She thought of Us as a contamination.

We were a force buried in Her, puzzling to Her, perhaps because of Her ignorance of Her own origin and of all the forces that were Her rightful heritage because of that origin.

2

Some men get a splinter in their heart and their heart becomes like a lump of ice. But Tara, since the time she had loved Nakul, had promised to melt all the ice with the warmth of her love. And there was a time he would believe her with his eyes closed. At first glance, Nakul seemed conventionally handsome. But there was always a faint self-disgust in his face, which marred the full fierce lustre of his brown eyes.

Tara dropped onto her back to take him in, so completely accepting of him. The intensity of his release brought him down to his knees and she was on her stomach and he took her again. There was a time he was scared of entering her child-like body; she told him it hurt, sharp at first, then awful, then contradictory, and when the pain became unbearable, it began to go away, changed and became something good to moan at; took over all the strength of his body.

"Did you like it?"

"You made me feel cheap," she said simply. said simply. Her eyes were brown and warm as summer earth. Her gaze direct and simple without art. There was a natural way about her that caused the dull ache in Nakul's chest to build with unexpected intensity.

"You showed your disapproval in a very strange way." He pointed at the scratches on his shoulders.

"Goodness!" Tara blushed hotly. "No! All I am saying is never make me feel cheap."

"I am sorry if I made you feel so." His voice was pleading and all her anger drained away. They were not adversaries. Their lives were hard enough without the hurt they might bring to each other.

"There is something troubling you. Why don't you just say it?"

"Where were you all day?" He asked in a certain tone of voice, and with a certain half-look.

"Nakul, this is the third time you're asking me and I have already told you—I went to meet my brother. Rodh narrowly escaped death and it is only because of Amba that he is alive. He was asking for you. You haven't visited them since Solon died. Tanu Bakar was there. He said they need more men out there."

"You seem to be unduly worried about his needs." The disgust on his face became more prominent at the mention of Tanu Bakar.

"You unduly mock Master Bakar. He has only been kind to us. Why do you not like him? I sometimes feel you hide things from me!"

He raised his hand to her lips to silence her. His young forehead, with its furrows of fretful and mysterious pain, advocated a present permanently circumcised by a dark past and it made him look older than his years.

"I don't care to hear about Tanu Bakar. I don't want any more talk about him or his freak group." He spoke with such an intensity that Tara looked up, startled.

"He only said they need more men. You must change your mind about leaving the Resistance."

"They have no need for someone like me. They have *her*." Nakul's voice again shook with the intensity of unexpressed emotions.

"What do you mean by that? And what will you do if not fight?"

"We will go away. Down to the plains. There is work there and we can start our life away from this useless war. I cannot sleep with weapons in my hands anymore."

Nakul gave an involuntary shudder. His nature recoiled from the grim work of war, but the truth was that he had hated the city too. He had been there once and found it too dark for his taste, a fathomless warren of concrete and litter and glass and alleys and tipping gutters and pavements spotted with trodden gum and filth.

"Abandon our people? Never. Remove that thought from your mind."

"Why not? The gods, too, have abandoned us."

"Don't say that."

"The gods of *Habishis* are nothing without fools who believe in them."

"Your ill health makes you speak like this. Will you go to the special ceremony? They are choosing the new squad leader."

"It's a stupid ceremony of a deluded freak group," he said as a man who feels his life closing in on him like granite walls.

"That's a horrible thing to say."

"You want the truth, don't you, woman? They have no chance defeating Madbull's men. We are like sitting ducks, waiting for our turn to be slaughtered. To be gutted like pigs."

Nakul knew he would never be operationally ready to be a militia man. A year ago, he had joined the fight against the state police regiment under Tanu Bakar, because he wanted to be seen as a *hero* too. Though, after a year of dodging death, he did not feel inspired anymore. Perhaps he never was, in the true sense. He was fed up of waking up every morning instantaneously grateful that he was in one piece and scared shitless because he was still in the same situation. He had started having nightmares of bombs and poison gas, of tunnels and gun wounds and rotting corpses. He wanted better dreams than those in which he kept falling into a hole and bodies piled over him and everything started exploding, and he was trying to fight back with no weapon and no ammunition. Nakul wanted to escape the death smell, the death rattle, the death talk, all of it. But most of all, he did not want to be anything like *her—his sister Amba*. He pitied himself acutely; felt ill-used and moving towards certain death.

Since last night something else had troubled Nakul. He had returned home to a strange sight. Not only did Tara seem annoyingly distracted, several unexplained gifts lay about in the house, including a handsome new calf in the courtyard with a round, white body and strong limbs and her horns pointing straight up. He told himself that Tara was not unfaithful, even though he had sometimes seen her laughing with men in the village. Nakul wanted to confront her, but was again limited by his somewhat circular nature. Being the opposite of Tara in nature, he did not come straight to the point. Nakul's temperament was both solicitous and self-doubting, attributes which, because they opposed one another, tended to engender in him a state of constant anxious flux. He began by saying all he ever wanted was what any man in love would desire: a wife who could withstand his tenderness, who didn't have the core of her locked away in a dark ocean; and that he wanted a soft moon in his hand, but today, he felt he was holding a scalding sun.

"You look distracted and distant. You look through me as if I am not here. What is going on?"

"Yes, my love," she said absent-mindedly. "Sorry—what did you ask me?" To his eye, she looked heavy with some guilty secret.

"I have never seen a woman look so happy when her husband is away. Unless someone else is keeping her happy!" said Nakul, glazing his eyes to indicate that he had only spoken in order to warn her. There was no reply at first. Only the air eating his words.

"You seem to have decided that I am guilty! What hope for me now when my own husband doubts me?" She mocked.

"You lied to me about that fat calf, which stands at our door, being a gift from your father."

Tara giggled. It was a tinkling noise, guileless, and he looked up, surprised. He did not expect her to laugh. Her body seemed to be wrapped in mothwing shadows, and her wet hair and freshly cleaned body and a milky baby smell summoned contrary emotions of love and jealousy in him. And he wanted to kiss *and* strangle her.

"You dare laugh at me after lying so brazenly! My head is bursting at the thought of what other lies you have uttered."

"Give your mind some rest. I have not told you any lies." She smiled, hugging her little secret closer to her chest.

"Don't pretend to be innocent. Who can be this benefactor who is being so generous to you behind my back?"

"My father—"

"Your father did *not* gift it to you," he jumped in. "I know because I asked him. You are turning into a liar! Now, why are you silent?"

"What am I to say when you have already labelled me capricious, fickle and immodest, and suggest I am of frivolous character? You absolve me of all sins, but with the next breath you spurn and revile me; you swear to adore me, yet you hurt me—for which I never gave you any cause."

In the strained silence that followed, Tara huddled in her corner of the bed, her eyes watchfully peeled at Nakul. Maddening thoughts, mottled and pin-headed like headless chickens resentful of captivity, would not stop running around screeching in his head, trying to poke their ugly, pointy beaks right through his heart.

"Don't use your womanly guile to get away now that I have caught you—"

"You sicken me! And since you *must* know—it is Amba's gift. She even named her. Coral. I know how stubborn you get when it comes to her, so I did not take your permission—"

It was Nakul's turn to be look bewildered.

"Yes! Your sister gave me the gift," she paused. "And this silver anklet, so I always know where she is. Amba was worried for me because she has seen how I stand in long lines every day to get milk and cheese and me being pregnant and all."

The words were a shock. Like, all this while her hands were empty and now, suddenly, she was showing a knife.

"You are *what*? Pregnant?" Nakul asked, his voice thrumming with charge.

"A blessing from the Goddess of Hori! I wanted to surprise you with the good news tonight!" she pouted.

"You confided in that cursed woman, who I am ashamed to call my sister, that you are pregnant and didn't tell me, your own husband!"

"I wanted to surprise you. And Amba is not a cursed woman."

"You are now learning to keep things from me. Is that cursed sister of mine teaching you this too? That witch!"

"Lie to you? No! She is only looking out for me. And she is no witch. At least, not a bad one."

"You have your husband to look out for you! Why do you need her? You should not have taken the gift. You better return it first thing in the morning."

"I will do no such thing."

"You will return that cursed woman's gift. For, nothing which comes from her can ever bear fruit. It will only bring ruin. We don't need her help. Am I not enough to take care of you? How many people do you need?"

"I will do no such thing. Your jealousy is making you lose your senses."

"Are you saying I am envious of my sister?"

"I am saying purge yourself of this grudging hate; get rid of it now, before it becomes an affliction!"

"You have lost your bloody mind, woman!"

"Stop shouting! You are frightening me. My person is not your property, even less my mind, that you can exercise whatever advantage is inherent in its ownership. Even if there is something about Amba, something we don't understand, she has never done us harm. She is your sister. Flesh and blood of our child."

"When I come back tomorrow, the calf shall not be here. Or I will take it to the butcher," he thundered, as if squashing some anticipated rebellion from Tara.

"Come back here—come back, right now! You cling to woebegone misery so fiercely and weirdly. Can't you see it's like a ghoul sucking your strength and our happiness away—"

Her comments were met by such a resentful glare, and a shrinking of his thin dry upper lip as if she had fingered his wound, that Tara stopped.

"Will there never be an end to it? To these fights?"

"Anything would be better than her charity. I don't need a cursed witch to look out for me. You are my wife and you must respect my wish. I don't want her taint to rub on our child. Get rid of it."

Even hours after the fight, Nakul would not stop shaking with resentment—and jealousy, though he would never admit it, and it made him redden with shame and indignation. There was not a thing he hated more than being reminded that he was *her* brother. The strange air she carried around her since they were small. A girl like her was not born because the gods felt extra kind to their family.

Odd, how certain things remain clear as crystal in the memory, brand new, shining as gold. People turning and staring and whispering about them. Always being whispered about. Neighbouring girls hulking, boys laughing, *Look, look, here's that weird girl's brother!* Those years of torment passed over him in a fever dream. The gossip about her; her difference—the sense of something bigger than all of them; that something which kept marking her for extra-ordinariness. And making him inconsequential and ordinary by comparison. Nakul knew that's how he would remain as long as she was alive. Inconsequential. Unless he did something about it.

⌘ TWENTY YEARS AND A DAY ⌘

We never house inside a weak vessel. Their mind slate remains soft, thought particles drop about as a watermelon on the pavement on a hot summer day. The bobble, the slip, the momentary suspension of time just before the hard rind ruptures and spills its fruit. Purposeless. Wasteful. It always ends badly for the weak vessel. There is another rule We observe. Once We house in a vessel, We don't abandon it. To make the vessel like Us is the extent of our intent.

Mother was always going to love the boy more. The boy revelled in the wild worship Mother served at his altar. He seemed to sense Her obligatory love towards him and grew in answering hardness. The boy was chubby, screamed a lot, and was moody and handsome. We sensed the weakness in him. The fragility. The selfishness. The cowardice. Lacking strong inner worlds, focused on the outside and at the mercy of the elements, he would never be selected by one of Us. Born and bred in the same womb, the brother and sister could not be more different.

Certain times, We got involved. Once, the brother, fascinated by the stone-god idols, sneaked into a temple. He touched the white porcelain skinned, ruby lipped and covered with pounds of shiny yellow, which was forbidden. The Village-Shaman caught him in the act and beat him with a rattan cane.

"How dare you stand in this line, you of impure blood!" He cursed and beat the boy till his skin broke and he ran home crying. We felt the strength of Her fury coursing through Us when She saw the blood on the boy, Her brother. She raced to the temple to confront the Village-Shaman. She pushed the shaman. It was the awkward shove of a young girl still not aware of Her true strength, but the Village-Shaman fell on his back, goggle-eyed and gibbering, in a way he never walked straight again. Then, he smelled Us inside Her. And he further shrank in fear.

Even at that point, We could have intervened and extracted sweet revenge once and for all, but She would not listen to Us. She wanted to be in control of Herself. It was a crucial line drawn.

She possessed something that did not come from Her father or Her mother.

She was unlike the vessels We had been in before. It was something put into Her soul when it was given life—the one different thing put in all, which made no two fingerprints the same. And We watched, intrigued.

She always was wary of Us. Did We have serpents for hair or scorpion tails and dripped blood? No. Perhaps She recalled a taste of Us from some previous life. Maybe She remembered what We could do. She watched Us, so as to never lose control over Herself.

We watched with grim pride as She lost awkwardness and gained, what people called, character. She became capable, hard and far-seeing. She exchanged Her tenderness for capability and a fierce desire for survival. She did not require anyone to tell Her there were other worlds besides the one She was born into. She would have to summon Us of Her own free will. For, only then, We were allowed to truly manifest ourselves. The difference from others got more marked with years. Even as a child, She sensed Her existence was tainted in some subtle, essential way. There were many times Her difference would stand out. She would not crawl like other human babies Her age; instead, she walked to get Her food on Her tiny limbs. We felt Her gape in delirious wonder at the green scent and profusion of life, which drifted from the Jotsoma forest. She would resist the urge to throw herself in, as free as a frog in a pond. She put it down to fear of the ferocious beasts concealed in the shadows. She was hesitant to discover the true nature of what lay housed inside Her. And instead of Us being the protecting layers, She served as an armour between Us and Her world.

We waited. The crossing itself was always extremely painful, and We were spent. We slept for decades, crouching deep inside Her bones and patiently biding our time, for the Pestilence was coming.

Soon, She would have no choice.

All We were to do was wait.

3

Moving with the economy of a mercenary, the man dipped his massive arm in a bucket of ice, his skin bristling all along his neck and back. He growled deep and low at the dappled snake. With a lightning move, he held it in a vice grip.

"Devil's spawn! Look at it go!" someone shouted. Moist, pink eyes pinned on its adversary, the snake's jagged-edged fangs struck again and again.

Little Death, as the snake was called, raised its fangs to deliver jabs of venom. But the man's face—evoking the mystery of an Olmec head—remained empty of expression. Cut from living rock; and from his back, his dark coat hung like wings jointed as a vulture's back. The puncture wounds looked inflamed, there was enough mycotoxin to kill an ordinary man.

But Rosie Madbull was no ordinary man.

Named after his mother, who died giving birth to him, Rosie Madbull was a man of brute strength. He once hoped to be a professional boxer. His skin rippled and his eyes were thin and slitted, his mouth a bloodless slash. When the snake stopped moving, he eased his grip and threw it in a cage, slamming it shut.

It was time for the show. The stage was set. Forty small houses had been combined to make the sitting area and fifty destroyed to make the central ground. The set-up presented a certain gladiatorial appeal, apt for the task at hand. Twenty-four young hopefuls awaited their fate. The instructor removed the white cloth covering a figure, revealing a naked corpse lying face down on the ground.

"Dismember the body," Madbull tasked the new boy.

The young aspirant's eyes widened as if he was not sure what he was being asked to do. "W-what…?"

"Is there a problem, boy?" Madbull asked, flicking his side-parted hair to the side with his massive hands.

"I am not feeling very good."

"Bad day to feel all balls, no cock."

"Uh huh—is this necessary? It is already dead."

"Boy, you know what they call me behind my back? Death. You believe that?" Madbull's cold, emotionless voice cut the air like a scythe.

"N-No…Sir."

"You should. You better. Now, do it."

Madbull ordered, touching the short-barrelled Slocum revolver in his waistband, a 5-shot .32 calibre. He carried it at all times, apart from the official firearms, for effect. He thrust a machete into the boy's hand.

"Are you going to pretend it is not easy to kill people?"

Standing over the body, the boy was trying to suppress an urge to vomit.

"Or are you going to say you did not expect to *actually* kill anyone!"

"Scaredy little wimps…don't have what it takes to be a Red-Hound," the instructor snickered.

"How many of you have killed someone before?" Madbull asked. A few nervous hands were raised, even as the instructor employing the word *ladies*, considering the company around, evoked howls of laughter. Colonel Madbull perceived himself as the arbiter of fate and operated outside of conventional understandings of justice and morality. He sometimes preached his philosophy before killing his victims.

"Little boys become officers. Get fancy haircuts. Your uniforms got creases. You got expensive guns on your hips. Suddenly, you want to go hard-core, but you actually are a fancy-schmancy power-point soldier. You pretend to be a meat-eater, but you piss pink mist at the sight of blood. What are you doing here? There is nothing unholy about maiming and blowing off men. War is not an eloquent blow to the neck or a jab to the heart. It is dirty, sticky, stinky, shitty, with blasted bodies, rotting parts, splattered brains, missing eyes, blown-off limbs, bloated intestines. Can you deal with it?"

"I don't know—"

Madbull fired a bullet into the boy's leg, who erupted in howls of pain as if crucified. The boy tried to cup the blood back inside his leg.

"Take him away. Did us all a favour," Madbull ordered. "Being a Red-Hound is an honour. Not everyone is suited to this line of work, so don't be stupid as to exaggerate your capabilities. It is about targets, boys. Man-shaped targets. It is about the death rattle and the targets foaming from the mouth, and the shaking and the shitting as they die. A 7.52 in the chest and pelvic girdle is too easy; he will be gone in a second. What is the fun in that?"

Next on, was a lanky boy. He held the blade like a trophy. He stabbed the corpse, determined to prove he was merciless.

"Open your eyes," Madbull ordered. The recruit slowly opened his eyes and stared at Madbull's expressionless, icy grey holes and a chill ran down his spine.

"No. Not at me. Look at *it*. Look. Strike." The runic angles of his clean-shaven face shone with sweat. The boy did not hesitate this time.

"Excellent. There is a good career for you, boy!"

Basking in the glow of admiration, and with renewed cruelty, the boy began swinging the scythe in all directions. He was one of the chosen few culled out today, for their cruel and ignoble disposition in the main, who would have to impress, by cunning and cruelty, and, if the occasion so demanded, by desperation of defence when cornered. The boy would now be the newest and the youngest member of the Madbull's private army—the Red-Hounds. Off the grid, because, for the state, they did not even exist. The main purpose for their induction into Madbull's private army was not revealed to them for it was of such a nature, which would never get state sanction.

"Bravo! You are on the path, now, to becoming a valuable member of the Red-Hounds. Welcome!"

Madbull was satisfied with his collection of mean, low, brutal fellows, which went well with his belief that one should be dispassionate and methodical in all killings. He was a firm believer in never giving up the chance to take a life.

The moment was soon to be interrupted by Mathera, his assistant, whom he had named the chief bearer of bad news: 'Prison Inspection Officer Nathan Ray had reached Baikaal'.

As it turned out, the mention of the name *Nathan Ray* caused Rosie Madbull's demeanour to change dramatically, and the very act of engaging in small talk became offensive. One need not even have to be particularly observant of human nature to gauge how, since the mention of the name Nathan Ray, different aspects of emotions gained and lost prominence, and the Colonel's face was transformed into a compound of fury and calculation at the thought of facing an old, and particularly persistent, antagonist.

"Should I set the snake free, Colonel?" asked the instructor, pointing at the cage.

"Give him to me," said Madbull. He held the angry but bruised snake gently. A purple dusk picked out jagged canopies on its dappled scales.

"Death should not be left wanting. Think of lust for the flesh," he said as he hobnailed over the creature. "Blood lust is like that. It should be fully satisfied."

4

Some people are born without a human conscience and those people need to kill. Prison Inspection Officer Nathan Ray firmly believed Rosie Madbull was such a man. An anonymous letter, detailing alarming goings-on inside the Baikaal prison, had reached him. The disjointed, incoherent complaint, to his eyes, was unquestionably genuine. Garbled and seemingly paranoid, the letter made a serious accusation against Madbull and, at one point, even said that Colonel Rosie Madbull was a 'fucking monster'. And that he behaved like a 'gang-lord' and had built a 'private army' of equally insane criminals, who had no business to be outside jail, and that 'some horrific crime' was definitely being planned, though it did not reveal the nature of the crime being plotted. When Nathan Ray failed to get permission for an official raid, he took it upon himself to corroborate the facts by making an unannounced visit to the jail in a vehicle designed as a delivery van.

Baikaal's putrid air and the sordid company made Nathan almost nauseous. To fob off the feeling, he emptied a bitter tincture into his mouth and reeled back in shock from the stab in his stomach. The jolt was intense, though it sobered him and banished the haze into a remote corner of his head. Soon, the adversaries stood face to face, eyeing each other warily.

"To what paltry pretences do I owe the honour of your visit?" Madbull's voice echoed off the stone ceiling, raw and baying. A hunting dog calling down its quarry. Nathan thought Madbull appeared more muscular than he remembered. Time had lent bulk to his chest and arms.

Nathan could almost imagine him with a whip in his hand, its metal tip rasping faintly as it dragged along the floor.

"Wish I could say it's been a pleasure."

"Our regular inspector, Mr Birjit Mamang, is suspended for bribery, I hear?"

"Illegal acts have consequences," said Nathan pointedly.

"And there should be, if one is stupid enough. Only lesser minds lose their sense in the presence of wealth. However, you are not here to discuss Birjit, are you?"

"A serious complaint has been lodged about the conditions at Baikaal."

"Activists are so sentimental! Their imaginations run riot. One should always suspect their description of the truth and not believe it without verification. I don't allow myself, or my men, to afford the luxury of sentimentality. Gambler's way to make a living, if you ask me," Madbull sounded almost normal, but Nathan knew better. He knew he was in the presence of a man who was directly animated by malice.

"He has complained about extreme torture by your men with your knowledge."

"All fiction."

"He has lost the use of his legs after the torture."

"How unfortunate. Still, it's not a death sentence. We don't torture at Baikaal. I would never authorise torture. Lack of imagination leads to sadism. Brute force is never the answer if the question is how to get cooperation. Brute force will get you lies, misdirection, bad answers. All the tools of medieval torture by the barbarians are of no use. Put a sack on a subject's head, wrap his hands in balls of gauze, plug his ears and drop him in a hole for a week, and you have a puddle of water. Is that torture?" Madbull's tone was heavy with sarcasm.

"To some, yes. I will find it extremely inhuman."

"Prison is not for everyone, especially not for the man of the mind," Madbull said, followed by "Who told you?", "There is no inhuman prison here", "That was in the past; in this better age, the old prison exists no longer" to "Everybody goes to jail these days", and finally conceded, "Prison is prison and prisoners are prisoners".

"If there is nothing to hide, why are the shredding machines working overtime—I cannot find any files on the convicts. Why are they missing if the files were only about necessary and routine interrogation of the guilty?"

"What do you think the files contained?"

"A good guess would be that the files were sprinkled with the names of interrogation officers, field agents, informants and community collaborators. You must know that you are supposed to cooperate with an officer of the state."

"My dear man, you are free to present whatever crushing evidence you have collected against me to the higher-ups. There is another committee above you for the more committed, and above that, another committee for the even more committed. And on and on, until you reach Uncle Ho himself, for all I care."

But even before Nathan could summon up a reply, he added, "You must also know that unannounced visits such as yours are completely unwelcome in my jail premises."

"The jail is not your personal property, though you seem to think otherwise. And, are you threatening me?"

"Never! But in a place like Baikaal, it's best not to make too much noise, or you get noticed by people, and many of them may not be tolerant. But did I say that? The only people who are a threat to our great country are the *Habishis*. Vermin. Pestilence."

Nathan bit back an ugly retort. He did not want to play into his gory script or end up contributing to his conspiracy stories.

"What do you plan to do?"

"Nothing outside the law. I will ask Mathera to take you on a tour through the confinement campus." Madbull's amused tone indicated that he wanted Nathan to admit to his hopeless situation of not getting anything out of him. "You can see for yourself. Baikaal is all yours! Goodbye."

Some people called the Baikaal prison a control mechanism for the entire prison system—a penal cesspool where other institutions discarded their waste. The ones unlucky enough to actually spend time whispered about the evil interiors, which controlled you forever. One could leave Madbull's jail, but one could never be free of him. Criminals, subversives, arsonists and, lately, activists, were specially sent to him to have their behaviour studied, punished or remedied. remedied. The thought of being 'remedied' by Rosie Madbull was enough to sterilise any thought of resistance. No one actually cared about how the deviants, psychopaths, criminals, the scum of earth, were treated behind the walls. It would have gone on but complaints soon poured in from a whole different segment of people—the activists. Madbull hated the 'activists' the most. He called them ungrateful vermin. They could be moderately benign intellectuals with decent jobs and a high education, who happened to have read banned poetry or taken part in some protest concert or listened to banned radio broadcasts; it could be anything. They were made to pay. They would go on paying. They would have to pay in full. In typical perverse fashion, he would 'talk to them'. Encourage them to ask questions which plagued them. Gave them a sense of hope, projected himself as their ally against the cruel state. Till they endlessly bemoaned their fates and covered every surface of their cells with scribblings about absurdity and injustice and cursed the state. The scribblings were carefully photographed and preserved as proof against their 'violent' mindsets. He played with them; while they spent a lot of time in red rooms, waiting for that phone call, that visit from friends or family, which never came. Many did not manage to finish serving the length of their sentences. Either they became deranged or killed themselves. Or got themselves killed, trying to escape.

Matters came to a head when one of them managed to straddle the prison wall, which was de-electrified during a power cut, thinking he would escape right into the jungle behind the prison. What he ran into was one hundred metres of barbed wire, sensors and hungry prison dogs having a free run down the corridors. The dogs took him down in no time. His maddening screams, as they tore into him, eating him alive, rang out for hours, and many thought the prison master deliberately delayed his rescue. By the time the guards got to him, there was nothing much left, except his head and a few fingers. Prison Human Rights Officer Nathan Ray was appointed to investigate the matter, and despite all efforts by Madbull and his men, proved to be impossible to impress or intimidate. Nathan's incriminating report found Madbull guilty of 'negligence' in the least and the Colonel was suspended for a period of five years. Angrily, Madbull blamed Nathan for his punishment posting in the remote Hori mountain outpost prison and spent months plotting and planning the suffering he would mete out to the man if he ever encountered him in a position of disadvantage.

But Rosie Madbull seemed to have the luck of the devil himself. His luck changed when traces of gold metal were discovered in the Hori mountain soil. Almost overnight, all complaints against the Colonel took a backseat. Making the most of the change in tide, Madbull eagerly employed his entrepreneurial skills and proceeded to make his deployment an extremely profitable enterprise by asking for a standard cut against a prospector license. No one was asking about the prisoners anymore. In the algorithm of commerce, they were inconsequential. No one, except Nathan Ray.

Baikaal was designed to subdue. Originally a monastery, the walls were made of rarefied concrete and the stone roofs were fifteen feet high, and mist floated in and out at whim, all during the day and in the night, giving it an eerie look. The eighty-three-acre compound was chopped into tiny cubicles, which were further sliced into miniscule cuboids. Mechanical grills and steel doors minced the concrete corridors into still smaller sectioned cubes, where a prisoners' line-up was pigeon-holed into a strict single file. Every few feet, a prisoner was stopped by a door. A ten-feet sojourn would have two stoppages and would take as many minutes, depending on how readily the inmate was granted permission to enter or exit.

It did not take him long to find out that the interrogation rooms were exactly as described in the letter: '*heard screams and sobbing at night; the guard let out that they were punishment rooms*', where inmates were '*hooded and brought for regular torture sessions, hounded about their allegiances, associates, accomplices and crimes*'. It had been used as a prison for political offenders for the past two or three hundred years, and its dungeon walls were scarred with the rudely carved names of many. He lost count of the number of times his heart sank, when he thought of the many captives who fretted their life away here and left no record of themselves but these sad epitaphs wrought with their own hands. The description of *'lights, which were left on forever, the cell where they almost died of sleep deprivation, the guards in electric-blue uniform, the bunks with the sink, bucket and a lone jug shacked to the floor with a chain'* tallied. He walked down the corridors where the *'inmates were made to endlessly prison walk, legs wide, hands high behind the back, head bent, till they fainted and would be woken up with steel batons'*. When Nathan received the anonymous letter, which graphically described the atrocities committed inside Madbull's prison, he could not simply sit back—the details were too specific to be untrue.

As the day drew to a close, Nathan's head felt stretched taut to its limit. He had not found any evidence of this mysterious *'private army'*, purportedly a gang of ruthless men committing illegal acts for Madbull. There were no visible openings to get at the truth and, despite trying his utmost, he kept running against a complete blank. For Nathan, there was nothing more exasperating than to feel a certain moral certainty of the guilt of a person and yet find the facts too feeble to bear testament to the same. But despite all his ferocity and coldness, there was an undercurrent of desperate intrigue that the Colonel seemed to be battling to subdue. He knew Rosie Madbull as a man who followed his own twisted moral code, one which was entirely a creation of his psychopathic mind; a man perennially wrapped in the cocoon of his own senses.

Nathan felt it all around him. Beneath the smooth, familiar face of normalcy, there existed something which was waiting to tear the world into two. He sensed it in the secret looks, in the hushed whispering, in the shredded files; the sense of something foul at play.

While he stood undecided at what to do, there came, from the direction of the basement, an inexplicable sound that rose to the volume of a woman's shriek.

5

"It's not fair, Master!" Sushithal was loudly petulant. "It cannot be!"

"Those are two different things, nephew."

"Amba cannot be allowed to lead us. You are making a big mistake—"

"Silence! You dare to doubt me, fool? You live as a favour to my sister. Do not test my patience is my advice to you, nephew."

Tanu Bakar's tone was explosive. Formidably tall, with an oversized nose and nicotine-stained lips, Master Tanu Bakar was mentally as sharp as a serrated knife. The sort who reached his own conclusions without regard for others' opinions. And he had made up his mind. No one else but Amba would lead the squad against the Red-Hounds. The one most upset with his announcement was his nephew, Sushithal, who, after years of training, fancied himself to be the best fighter. Though Tanu Bakar loved his sister's son, he knew Sushithal was not a great observer of the human nature. It came from a fundamental blindness to all experiences other than his own. Sushithal was shocked Amba was chosen over him and it was partially to do with nurturing the belief that women could not lead militia.

"Does anyone have any more objections?" Tanu Bakar asked and glanced at Nakul. The few times their eyes met, a slow, dull resentment seeped out of him, like coal gas, thin and sour. He averted his gaze.

"But how can we have one such as her lead?" Sushithal complained again. "It is bad enough that the Resistance needs the services of someone like that. People from other villages will laugh at us."

"One *such as her*? You seem to have been spending too much time listening to old wives' tales, you fool. And the greater fool, you, that you bring it up when we are discussing serious business. If I was not sure earlier, nephew, I am sure I made the correct decision, now."

Tanu Bakar refused to be confounded with Sushithal's resentful and revengeful tone condemning his decision, for he knew that criticism is only suppressed envy. Spite-covered faces, stamped with simmering arrogance and barely concealed violence, visible in the eyes stuck on faces plump with arrogance.

"Most of the fellows are scared of her— C'mon, speak up?" Sushithal nudged the rest, standing in a restless circle.

"They won't, you fool. Because each one of them, and you too, know that Amba is the best we have in combat. I don't care where she gets it from and I don't care what they say about her—and neither should you—but I am ready to even take Patala's help if it can get rid of the Red-Hounds' pestilence."

The air could be cut with a knife at the secluded militia garrison, which projected a deceptive state of normalcy. Two years ago, the Resistance group against the state police did not exist, except in Tanu Bakar's head. He built it from scratch; assembled a group of young *Habishi* fighters, trained them in ambush-combat, warfare and use of heavy artillery among other things. He made strict rules. No fighting. No disrespecting. No ratting. No cowardice. No hard drugs. Discipline was strict and punishment hard. The militia training camp was flanked on the right by an almost-vertical overhanging rock face, and on the left, by arroyos consisting of fluid sediment, and prone to rockslides and difficult to breach, unless one knew the exact route. The garrison was spread out in a sheltered lower ridge on the western Jotsoma, rendered virtually invisible to an approaching enemy due to its unique geographical location. It was instrumental in producing well-trained armed fighters, served as the biggest line of defiance to Madbull's men, and in doing so, Tanu Bakar managed to consolidate his position as the 'Master', hugely respected and feared.

Tanu Bakar's demeanour reflected the desolation of his land, the grimness which belongs inevitably to a country plundered of its men and swept with the ruinous winds of greed and injustice and rebellion and petty squabbles. He was a man who lived under the weight of the proud uniqueness of the destinies of his people, the *Habishis*, buried under the compromises of how many years, he had lost count. He had fierce love for his land but he felt shame at his peoples' repeated exploitation. Every time he thought of the wealth his people ought to have commanded, as natural owners of the land, he felt a swell of anger in his chest; an anger so bitter, it manifested in physical pain. Once upon a time, the people commanded the entire western Hori mountains, from the steep-sided fjords in the east to the stony mountains on the left. But several years ago, the government had taken over extensive tracts and the most fertile land, reserving for them only the Iravati river, sections of its banks, and parcels of land near the foothills of the mountain. The *Habishi* villagers had, evidently, quite misunderstood the conditions upon which the land had been given to them. It was daylight robbery by the state, but the people meekly accepted the deal. Then the cursed 'miracle' occurred. Gold metal reserves were discovered in the mountain soil and, from then on, keeping their land became a constant and increasingly dangerous struggle. The attacks were more brutal, since the people rebuffed the state's offer to relocate again. The situation had worsened in the last few weeks. He knew their chief threat consisted of the sly and treacherous manner in which the enemy was attacking them, and he could not but help feel they were moving in the direction of some horrible danger. Adept in duplicity and deceit, Madbull's men had taken to employing organised subterfuge across villages. People were informing on each other and the reward for getting 'information on the Resistance militants' was being trebled. Civilian volunteers were being coerced to join the regiment patrollers invading the houses of *Habishi* sympathisers. His great fear was, if an offer was timed right, the authorities could get almost any information from the new recruits; some hardly worked the fields, others typically loudmouthed and the rest trigger-happy, flaunting their gold chains and guns.

"This is unfair!" Sushithal, like an obtuse fool who does not know when to stop, bleated in loud disappointment. "Days of taking fire, dodging RPGs, finding IEDs...And what do I get? This is not fair, Master! *I* should be the first choice—in fact, I am the best choice to lead the squad. I have no problem with her fighting under me." *More bodies. More deaths. More ammo. Bigger hero.* It was simple logic in his head.

"That's enough, you fool!" Tanu Bakar raised his hand and smashed it down as he took possession of all he surveyed. Though many in the crowd could not hear the words he said, the force and the meaning of them was clear.

"Whatever anger any of you have over my choice, keep it to yourself. It is only I who decides who is at what position in the Resistance. And I have decided Amba will lead the squad."

"I was just saying it's not normal for women to lead militia…or maybe, it's not the job for *normal women*!" Sushithal muttered softly, the air eating most of his words. He winked weakly at his friends in a bid for reciprocity, but they avoided his eyes to avoid appearing too sympathetic. Finding himself isolated, Sushithal got further enraged. He hated being made to look like a fool, which was often, and like any bully, soon turned his attention towards the weakest.

"Pretty boy—" Sushithal swaggered with a false bravado to Nakul, who was sitting in a corner, and addressed him loudly, "What are *you* doing with real soldiers? Your sister is enough man for both of you! Isn't she, fellows? Boy, you should stick to practising targets on paper and plastic."

"Leave me alone. I am leaving the Resistance. I have informed Master—"

"Leaving! Boys, did you hear that! The pussy is running away since he found out the Red-Hounds aren't made of paper and plastic!"

"I don't want to fight with you."

"Fight with me? You coward, I don't fight with little girls pretending to be boys."

"Please. I am not here for any trouble—" Nakul said stiffly.

"*I-don't-want-to-fight-with-you!* What a coward!" Sushithal mimicked Nakul. "Whatever did our lovely Tara see in you—"

"You are drunk. Aren't you?"

It was Amba. She drew her gun and placed the muzzle between Sushithal's eyes. Hers was the chilling expression of a person who has spent enough of their life stuck in hard rain and cold fog. Waiting for artillery and relief, stuck in the cold drizzle air, and out, the hot, painful breath, stuck with no morphine and little sleep, and surrounded by bodies, rotting parts, splattered brains, missing eyes, ripped limbs, bloated intestines. All around, men fingered their rifles nervously.

"Yes…yes." For the first time, Sushithal's voice shook.

"In that case, I will not shoot you, if you apologise to Nakul right now—"

"I don't need your help." Nakul seethed. His younger sister's concern clawed at his ears. Any other time and every other time, in all his years, he would have curled upon himself and wept. That day, the scornful looks were a spark falling on dry tinder.

"I am just trying to help."

"Help yourself. You all stink of weirdness, specially you—" Nakul took a step towards Amba. "Stay away from Tara," he hissed, a surge of fury possessing him before he walked away. But he did not get far.

Braaaaaaaakkkkkkkkkkkkkkk!!!

It seemed every gun in the city had gone off.

From downtown to the hills, light weaponry and flurries of orange tracers swirled into the sky with the suddenness of a blood-curdling war-whoop. A thunderous noise erupted on both sides of the river, which meant they were completely surrounded. Muzzle flash rippled on the far side and the boom of grenades rent the air as several tree trunks shattered in a hail of splinters and sparks.

When the grenade struck, Amba's limbs seemed to turn to molten iron from the heat of the blast. All she would remember later were the metal scraps flying, shards of broken glass, burning rubber and her suffocating in the sooty air, and then, something black plunged down from the heavens, straight on her face, and a strong hand pushed her on the ground. Tanu Bakar tucked his rifle under his arm, produced a cloth and began to bind the howling man's wounds. Another shell screamed—a storming banshee over huddled heads landed on the grove, exploded, and flung the earth into a red mud storm and a shower of pine needles. Bullets whistled through among the branches and nipped at the trees. Twigs and leaves and early snow came sailing down and the men constantly ducked and dodged the wooden hail. One of their victims swayed about without his hands, looking comical, as if was an escapee from some macabre theatre. A whip snapped near Amba's ear. The next moment, Gora's skull snapped open into red chrysanthemum and she ducked. Something wet sprayed her face and she knew, from its fresh coppery smell, it was blood. What began as an intermittent splutter of mortars, was now a flurry of artillery. Being on the bank's downward slope saved them from the main brunt of the ambush by keeping them below the eyeline of the assaulters. Tanu Bakar yelled at them over the sound of the fireworks, flashing and thumping in the sky all around.

"More of them are coming! We are surrounded!"

And sure enough, a red-and-blue swarm of men came on, swinging their rifles at all angles and yelling shrilly. The battery charged at full, and scattered and slaughtered the few hapless scouts caught off guard.

Amba's companion was hit on the mouth, and blood covered his face, even as he tried to childishly cup it back into the hole on his head. She helped another man, whose intestines hung from the back—such was the force of the bullets which had ripped through him—and further on, another, who stood under a tree, his knee joint splintered by a ball. The mortar inside the kerbstone exploded; one, and then the other. She dropped to the ground to protect her face. Hiding behind the fallen tree, she heard the bullets snap over her head. A grenade exploding close to the head messes up the mind. Her sense of reality became thin.

After the gunfire subsided, the evening possessed a surreal quality. The charred and colourfully mashed up people on the road added to the impression. The mood was eerily relaxed. And, for some time, she thought they could all escape. Even when the weight of a knee fell into her back and pushed her deeper into the sand, she believed. That all of them would be able to escape somewhere safe. Not until she felt someone tightening steel cuffs onto her wrist did she begin to doubt. Rough hands pushed her into a vehicle and she conceded for the first time, she was being taken and she was on her own.

Nakul felt the flesh over his heart grow thin, and his first instinct was to flee when the first spattering of gunfire burst. The crack and roar and thunder and the suddenness of the attack struck fear in him—and then, from beyond the blank hill, the snarling of soldiers and the clank of their metal accoutrements squatting as savage chief's guns turned on him, barking deadly orders. He expected to be hit by a bullet in the throat or the mouth and cold drops of terror started to form on his brow. But then he was spotted. Fear rapidly encased him in hot lava.

Blood rushed up his throat and he ran as fast as he could, knocked his shoulder heavily against a tree trunk and fell headlong. Grievously hurt from the fall, he collapsed several times. IEDs hurtled over his head with long, wild screams, grinning at him with bared teeth. He tore off sprays from barks of trees. He ran through slippery gullies choked with blade-thin witchgrass, stumbling over objects falling on uneven tracks, clambering over fallen trees. In his mind, he could hear the howls of derision at his desertion. He looked about for a place to hide in, some dark place where they would not get to him. Finding a cavity big enough for a slender man, he crawled inside. From his hiding, he peered down at the long lines of vehicles leaving the mountain. Their lights stared back at him with their multiple lidless windows of a night beast. The adrenalin dropped and he felt the sun and the close heat of the mountain. His legs ached and his eyes hurt, the stench of smoke and burning flesh stuck in his throat. This smell would never leave him, he knew that.

Shells came swirling again and exploded in the grass, or disappeared among the trees, to become strange war flowers bursting into fierce blooms, and a burning shrapnel skimmed the flesh of his arm. He felt his flesh bubble. It resembled a roasted fruit. His voice shrivelled in his throat and was scorched to dust. The pain was such he never imagined could exist. The pressure on his chest was a beast, pushing ash down his throat and nose as he fled. A blistering sweat broke out and his eyeballs were about to crackle. The heat of hot stones filled his nose and the shame of his impotent rage filled his mouth at being a pathetic coward.

She was gone. Gone. Her smell, her sight, her flesh and bones. Assaulted, blindfolded and taken away in front of his eyes, while he silently watched. He had let them take her. His own gutlessness was a repeated knife in his heart; self-loathing hit him and hot tears of remorse streaked his cheeks. Stumbling blindly, he ran till the sun petered out of focus and bats flitting in the darkness gathered in the forest.

As silence returned, Nakul cried softly to himself, then he cried loudly in pitiless desolation that ringed him around; and, for a long time, he was shaken by great, dry sobs.

It was dark, and smelled of dead bodies in the hole, but that was where he spent the night and the next day, trying to reconcile with his cowardice. What he struggled not to acknowledge was the feeling of growing relief at being finally rid of her.

⌘ MOULTING ⌘

It was inevitable She would continue to move in a way that had nothing to do with Us. She would get embroiled in human battles and wars which We did not understand or really care about. Nor could We predict or have foreknowledge of the outcome of the wars She would wage.

She would always have human frailties. Her human skin soft, easily punctured, marked, drowned, set on fire, ravaged. She would be scarred, gouged in places, bleed. She would feel pain and We would feel Her pain. But We could not intervene. Because there is no binding yet between Us and Her. We are limited by the constraints of the human vessel. Once inside, We are subject to Her human condition.

Trapped inside, We could do little if She refused to summon Us.

She thought of Us as some parasite with many heads. We had no choice but to fall back and stay curled up deep inside Her, dormant. Yet Our presence continued to shape Her temperament and skills. We could feel the unsettling Our mere presence caused Her.

But there is now a shifting of worlds. An unwholesome thickened air coats everything with an oily heaviness. A foul, seeping contagion. A miasma. Pollution of spirits. It rose from unpurified crimes, from unsanctified spilling of the blood. We sense a moulting. It would take time, but She would shed Her old form and become Her true self. And there would be consequences.

It was a new thing, tasting this feeling of uncertainty, of change, She felt. An unchartered taste. The Frenzies and Furies and Rages were hungry, ready and waiting for Her summons when She sheds Her old form. We are curious to see how much She would be ready to bear before She called out to Us.

6

The crowd gaped at the young *witch*. They wanted her to cry. To beg for mercy. To beg for her life. But she remained an indifferent spectator of a world gone mad. When she seemed to smile, it infuriated them.

"How could the chit of a girl, so beaten and bruised, show no fear?" they whispered to each other, enraged. They kept stalling the procession in restless circles as the Red-Hounds dragged her through the slurry-filled roads, all the way to the Baikaal prison.

It was not she who was scared. The crowd saw that. And it startled them.

"Is that a witch?"

"Looks like an ordinary girl. Nothing special!"

"If she were a witch, wouldn't we have been struck yet?"

"Exactly. I think those villagers are lying."

"She is definitely no witch. Girl is a fraud, if you ask me."

"I don't know much about witches, but I do know no witch can be paraded so without things happening. She is a lying troublemaker."

"It's proved. This is just a girl and I will lay her! Rut her like a dog. Isn't that how these soldier girls love to fuck?"

When some boys teased her, she looked almost amused, as if she had nothing to do with the hysteria to banish her to a fate worse than death. She stared glazed-eyed at the feral-eyed children who, aping their crazed fathers, jabbed at her with mouldy firewood sticks. A stout, rotund-faced farmer hit out towards her with a whip. There were little knots in the lash to make it sting more and it caught her cheek and drew blood. The assailant caught her attention, and the look in her eyes made him freeze.

By the time the procession arrived outside the gates of the prison, the air was heavy with misshapen clouds blotting out the sun. The murky sky soon transformed into a playground of bestial couplings of clouds, portentous of some primeval event.

Baikaal seemed an emblem of perdition itself. A blast of corruption, just like the stench exploding from rotting flesh emanates from inside. It took all of Amba's courage to walk upright when she heard the metallic clang of the heavy iron doors close behind her. She found herself instantly enveloped in an explosion of sound and stench, coalesced together in a vile clinging wetness, a shifting cosmos of filth. For Amba, the need to bathe in scalding water was instant.

Hers was a special cell, segregated from the rest. Sordid, thick, greystone monastic walls, brackish with age, a reinforced door, and inside, a steel mug and tray chained to the floor, and an iron bunk, with a half-inch piece of foam wrapped in coarse plastic strapped across, that was supposed to act as a mattress for the iron bed. It cut into her back; the customised pattern imprinted, she woke up several times, disoriented and drained. High on one wall was a small window that admitted a sliver of light for half an hour in the morning. The window itself was covered with pigeon shit, which cast its sickly yellow hue on the world outside.

Whip, her dog-faced guard, took special relish in informing her that since she had been designated as a 'dangerous inmate', she was subject to a different set of rules from the other inmates, including zero contact. And then there was the 'inspection rule', wherein she was made to kneel for hours, naked, on the ice-cold floor for the physical inspection, which was prolonged and humiliating. Whip, short and solidly built, with a buzz military cut, looked sort of a man who lived for moments like these.

Every twenty minutes, Whip's torch washed over her, halting its arc, at repeated intervals, verifying, examining, confirming, checking, preserving her, a specimen in amber. And if she was not in the 'sleeping position', it was followed by punishment. Deprived of water, the persistent reverberation of metal doors opening and closing now sent a searing pain up her head, till it throbbed and pounded, ready to burst. Relentless thirst kicked off a defence mechanism and her body responded by becoming progressively numb. Feelings became indistinct, emotions unpredictable. In the throes of delirium, soon she was past caring; time was ductile and malleable, bent and doubled, and she stumbled from day to night to day, time fused into a continuum.

Late that night, Amba awoke to rough hands blindfolding her. Managing to push one hand loose, she fought back, and got a nail in, ripping downwards as she met flesh. A scream of pain. Followed by a punch on her breast that knocked her breath out. Next, she found herself in an underground cell, which smelled metallic cold and dank. The only sound was the echoes of their footsteps. The blindfolds off, she saw her breath by the light of bare bulbs. She had heard about it from an old inmate, about the zero light, stress position isolation room. She glanced upwards, visualising where the rooftop water tank was positioned four storeys above. Her gaze followed old pipes along the ceilings to the cells. At first, she could barely make out the heavy wooden block of the contortion seats. The chains. Hundreds of them. Chains dangled off ceiling, walls, with leather linings and with nails jutting into the tiny, rusty enclosures, some with heavy iron balls attached, few with spikes radiating into the centre. The woodgrain looked smooth and polished, the kind you get from constant rubbing with human flesh.

The sudden icy blast of rusty water struck her in spurts, leaving her gasping. Bits of iron grated her chest and the taste of zinc, of metal rain, gutter water with the smell of fall leaves, freezing bricks and mortar seeped in, not bad or good, just familiar. Because she could not endure the moments as they ticked by, her mind travelled to faraway places. The floor was wet, cold. Icy. A moment later, she heard the screech of the old valve. And it hit her again in a great, icy gush. The water was cold and alive. And it bit. Her body started to go numb and she fell back into the water with a hideous spray. Her ears were full of the sound of her own erratic thumping in the chest, as if a bird were trapped inside her ribcage and was beating herself to death.

"Get up, witch woman!" Whip kicked her on the head.

Blood from the cut on her head gathered in her eye and seeped in, blinding her vision. The rest trickled down the cheek. Partially blinded, she saw Whip's belt swinging towards her. She lifted her head an inch and dragged her body forward on her belly, trying to not to expose her hands, on which the guard liked to stamp. Whip heaved back, gathered pace, and threw another vicious kick. It knocked Amba's breath out. Huge chunk of flesh, from her armpit to the wrist, was on fire, and she felt a pain so terrible, she cried shamelessly for mercy.

Incoherent with pain, she screamed. Then, crumbled to the ground and lay still.

Whip, now slightly worried, brought his hand near her nose. At first, he could not feel her breath. Then, Amba winced; there was no separate pain she could pick out. He let out another curse, plump with relief, beer, blood and piss.

"See what you made me do? Let this be a lesson, mongrel."

He smelled of unwashed men sweating with anger. Inch by inch, she moved, head down, her nose clotted with blood, mouth open to breathe; instead, she vomited.

"Shit, spew your shit, now! You should eat it right back, mongrel."

It hurt so much she wondered if her neck was broken. Breathing was difficult. That did not mean anything, she told herself, it was only because of the clotted blood inside her nose. Amba turned her head sideways, her hair soaked in her own vomit. Her head lolled helplessly on the spinal cord. She felt a movement under her. The ground became the Iravati river, it gave and swayed and, with a great gasp, opened into a deep, cold, black abyss, and she was pulled down and down and down with the deep, black tide. Her mouth was slightly agape. There was an angry bluish-purple bruise upon her temple and her cheekbone looked painfully swollen on the place she was struck violently. Gagged, blindfolded, her screams reduced to drugged grunts.

"She had better not be dead. Have you even fed her, you fool?"

The voice was a whiplash, a rapid staccato of words from someone used to giving orders. The man nudged Amba's near-senseless body with the tip of his boot and watched her hand curl and clasp at nothing.

"All drama. She is acting. Believe me, she is a strong one—dangerous too—we have to be careful around her," said Whip.

Crouched in a stress position, with hands stretched behind her back and legs tied, Amba faced her self-appointed inquisitors. Sweat flowed freely under her back as the accumulated heat made her breathless and flushed. Whip propped her up and splashed cold water on her face to wake her fully. Rough fingers prised open her mouth and a rice ball was shoved inside, followed by potato mash. Raving hunger pangs made her gulp it all down, even as she surveyed her surroundings. Her eyes were the very cloak of darkness and she moved her bruised limbs with the murderous languor of a caged panther biding its time.

7

Rosie Madbull sat quietly sipping water from a bottle, watching the blood streaking from the corner of her forehead. She was being eyed. She was being assessed. It was being gauged of her—*was she a witch*? The menace about him was palpable.

"She doesn't look like a witch," he said dismissively.

"Blood that can be made to flow so easily cannot belong to a witch," Mathera quipped in.

"You fools should have concentrated on getting Tanu Bakar. What use is this pathetic lowly creature to me? She is a damn con-artist."

"They talk about her at the village. She is a strange one. Trained in combat."

"If the world did contain the power the villagers allege, do you think it will fall on one such as her to discover it?" Madbull looked directly at Amba. She remained silent.

"Answer him, *witch*!" Whip prodded her painfully with his boot.

"Tanu Bakar even sent her to a college in the valley. Is it not true, girl?"

Whip kept glancing with inquiring sympathy at his master.

"Is Tanu Bakar your trainer?"

More silence.

"Mongrel girl, answer!" A vicious blow on her face sent her crashing to the ground.

"Tanu Bakar is a deserter from the Regiment. Did you know that? He was a good soldier at one point of time, before he turned traitor like all you bloody *Habishis*. I will make sure he is put down like the cowardly dog that he is."

"He is no trai—" Amba began to speak, but Mathera slapped her hard, his ring catching her on her ears. Hot tears of pain rolled down her cheek and she felt nauseous. She kicked back and her attacker fell down. She held him off near her knee, looking like a night beast, and could have done serious damage if she was not tied.

"Let her speak."

Madbull commanded and both Mathera and Whip shrank into the shadows. Amba took in the gathering with her odd-shaped, almost perpendicular pupils, ancient and bottomless, and not of any one constant colour. Her gaze seemed to beheld everything, the men's depths and dregs, all their hidden ignominy and ugliness. Madbull looked away, perhaps scared of getting sucked inside.

"What were you saying, girl?"

"Tanu Bakar is a honourable man. Your men are thugs in uniform."

Mathera's fist would have caught her on her eye. But she ducked, and its hard knot caught her eyebrow and opened another cut. She held her ground. Her absence of fear baffled them.

"Get up, mongrel," ordered Whip, his eyes working out where to kick Amba next.

"Is this the best of Tanu Bakar's crop? That slippery old fox escapes every time…but not for long. He deserted you, too. The true nature of vermin parasites we are dealing with. You people are locusts and will be destroyed. Can you not see the future, witch? I heard you have special powers!"

"You heard wrong," Amba said.

"I hear you can lift grenades with your hand and not die. That's something the bravest of men will not do."

Stubborn silence.

"I have heard you don't fear death, witch?"

"How can I answer for those whom you talk of?"

"Do you have any special powers? Will you cast a hex if you get angry? Frankly, isn't it an enormous impossible strain, following in the footsteps of the beast? I have nothing against witches and such. You know why?"

A fixed smile upon his swarthy face, and his bulging eyes like of men corrupted by a malevolent hatred and rage, Madbull said, "Because irrational defines your kind. Since you have gone to college, you will understand what I say. You people, there is no recognisable principle of justice. The *Habishis'* intellect is very basic, crude, vulgar, animalistic. If your kind are allowed to own this land, it will be the triumph of barbarism over order."

"All you want is to ravage our land for metal under our mountain and *we* are the barbarians? A whore, selling her body for few dimes, knows more about honour than you!"

Madbull had sat motionless throughout this indictment. His face, somewhat pale, was drawn into lines of deep fury, but he permitted her to finish, without interrupting.

"Ah! Our land, our land, our land! Why do you always talk of the land? And you blame *me*? You people don't respect the law and your hate builds up till the floodgates open, and either you all take a gun to the civilised people, or you get swept away by perversions and go mad. This hatred for justice and order cannot be allowed in civilised society."

"You asked me a question. If I have special powers. I have. And so does every *Habishi*, even the frailest of women, even our old men, even the *Habishi* child. We all have it. And you will have to face that if you try to take our land."

"So when you are thrown out, what are your people going to do? Take to the river in leaky little boats?"

"For all your logic, you live in more terror of the dark, don't you?" Amba's taunt infuriated Madbull.

"Live in the terror of the dark? I am the fucking god of this motherfucking mountain, you witch!"

"There is still time. All we want is to tend to our land. You want to own the land, ravage it, destroy it. We will always stay here because we are the children of Hori. You will go after you have eaten as much as you can off her. We cannot let that happen. Take your people and leave."

"The witch commands me! You heard that, boys!" said Madbull and the corners of Amba's lips curved up in a smile.

"What is so funny, witch?" asked Madbull, confounded by her fearlessness.

"I laugh at your ignorance and your stupidity. You are just a cunning blend of atoms—no different from what the *Habishi,* who you hate so much, too, is made of—and yet, you huff and puff for a set period of time; and the time will come, when the machine will be handed a command, by its own cells, to stop working." Amba wanted to stop speaking, but the rage inside her had a life of its own.

"How dare you talk like that—" Whip kicked her and promised worse fate at night.

"No, let her speak. She is college-educated, after all," said Madbull.

"Then, hear this. Your power means nothing. When your time is up, you won't be able to stop your own cell from commanding your body to stop all functions. And that command, by that inconsequential cell, will be obeyed by all the other cells; they will stop working. But I laugh more, that a man should think he knows what death is. Imagine what the pains of death are, when the whole body is corrupted and dissolved; when many times death pass, with less pain than the torture of a limb; when death will be, but, mercy for you."

Her words sounded like a curse and a prophesy—of events being set into motion. That night, Rosie Madbull would dream of her. That she spat on his human hide. It rippled and came alive, and she stretched it from one shoulder blade to another, draping it over her back and stitching it to another skin. And fashioned him into a different animal. He would wake up sweating and thankful that she was in his jail.

It would be a long night for Madbull, but he did not know it yet.

Whip was back in her cell. Looking more murderous than before. And drunk. He nudged Amba's chest with his leg. Poked her with the pointy snout of his studded leather boot and pressed its heel against her chest. He kept nudging her, refusing to let her sleep.

"This is what happens to girls who pretend to be witches. Remember, you are just a cunt."

Whip's foot nudged her once more. She smelled his distinct gamy odour. She trembled.

"Please. Let me sleep," she pleaded.

"You won't tell me what to do, mongrel bitch," Whip prodded her viciously with his foot.

That foot, its interrogatory tap grated, poked, cut against her skin over and over again. That foot, if only she could cut it off. The demon foot, which would not let her rest. Its horned toes scraped the flesh off her thigh, back, hip, shoulder. That foot knew whenever she was on the verge of sleep and returned at that moment to rob her of that last piece of sanity. Not being allowed to sleep was the demon eating her alive. It was the constant wakefulness which was unbearable. The only interruptions to mark the passage of time were that foot and the occasional touch of hands, lifting her hood and squirting water down her throat.

The foot became the main demon now. Her judge, jury and executioner. Rubbing into her with its sharp nails, its calluses, its meanness, its pettiness, taking out its raw deal on her flesh, the foot became suddenly more terrifying than rape, than hunger, than death. More powerful than a bullet. She woke up again from her half-asleep state to Whip tugging at her hood. His breath smelled of hog and sawdust, for he worked in a slaughterhouse for many years.

"I want to sleep. Just let me sleep," she pleaded.

"You know very well I cannot let you sleep," Whip snarled. "I must access the safe hiding the last of your secrets."

"What do I confess to?"

"If I told you what to confess to, it won't be much of a confession, huh?"

A silence ensued, until the foot nudged her again.

Lack of sleep made her eyes throb. A clammy tongue, swollen to twice its size, and her head in the pincer grip of a monster headache. Half-awake, her limp body was dragged to another cell. Arms pinioned, she lay helpless, spreadeagled on the floor. A foamy material was wrapped around her hands and feet and a hood was pulled over her head. She stopped squirming. She wanted to focus on the breathing through the hood. Was she alone now or was someone watching her? How many would rape her? Would they kill her later? Thousands of hungry thoughts crawled into her head like cockroaches and she shivered in revulsion.

Her eyes covered, Amba felt a bunch of men around her. Trousers removed, they caressed themselves in anticipation. One of them unbuttoned her shirt and stripped it off her. A hand untied the cord holding up her pants and pushed them down around her ankles. Another hand pulled at the knot fastened around her wrist and ankles. Moaning, she retracted her legs and curled into the tightest ball.

Amba couldn't see much from behind the cover on her eyes. There was some more cautious breathing. A shadow moved on top of her. She stopped thinking when the man penetrated her. A great gush of bile shot up her throat as thick, rough fingers moved over her stomach and lingered on her breasts. The man paused to test the strength of the rope. Another man took his place. There was no point in struggling. She waited for the rape to end. A line of acid slid down her throat and traced through her stomach. Through the hood, all she saw were shadowy faces, bright as whetted blades. Multiple hands groped her breasts. A muffled, deep voice commanded her to shut up and stay still.

"See? I told you all. She is no witch. Just a tight cunt."

"You hear you are lucky? The Colonel wants you alive."

"Man, I came so fast!"

"It's my turn…"

"Not fair, I should have got my chance, too."

"Have patience…Tomorrow, by this time, no little *Habishi*'s popping out of this one anymore."

"Look at her eyes! How she stares!"

"Are you casting a curse on us, witch?" voices mocked and taunted.

"You will know soon, won't you?" Amba hissed back.

"Witch, if you *are* one, how can I touch you and kick you and you cannot do anything about it? You are no witch!"

"She is just a cunt. Look at all I do to her!" The man placed his meaty hand on her breast and kneaded it roughly.

"Maybe she is liking it!" he said and the others cheered. Amba thrashed against the constraints. One of the men, whose fingers were near her lips, screamed in agony. Amba spat out the severed finger. The blood that trickled from her mouth was not hers.

"Aaaaaaaaaghghhhh!! Bloody witch has bitten me…she has bitten me! My finger…it's burning…on fire!" his agonising screams filled the room.

"Put a cloth over this mess. Now see what you have gone and done."

Eyes ablaze, Amba laughed and dared the men to come closer.

"Get the needle. She will behave soon. Everyone does." They tried to act cocky, though there was a hint of fear now. Her retaliation had drawn a fierce line.

"I can smell your fear, you dog," Amba seethed, not knowing where the courage came from.

"Cockteaser mongrel! I will prove that you are just a cunt." The man said angrily and hit her hard on the face.

She licked away the blood that followed the blow; and, fixed upon the offender with cold composure, her eyes seemed to say, "You will die for that."

"Her eyes! Her eyes! Cover her damn eyes! Blind the witch. I have heard their power is in their eyes," said someone, and another inserted foam plugs into her ears and inside her mouth, followed by a cloth, and jabbed her with a needle.

Blow after blow he struck, till her cloth was soaked with blood. The blood and the beating must have grown tedious after some time. Or maybe her assaulters remembered their comforts and the liquor and the food and their women waiting for them at home and, one by one, they drifted off. Dried blood caked her ears and nose from a concussion. She felt sick and dizzy and could hardly hear. Her body was sore and aching from the brutal hurt inflicted.

She lay on the floor lifelessly as dark changed to dawn, crunched in a foetal position, too scared to move a muscle, even when she was alone. A wiring loosened in her head. It set free soundless memories. Old memories. The memory of the blood trickling down Mother's legs leaked in. She had been raped by several men, but Amba, then just a little girl, had no idea then what rape was. She was frozen with the fear of a child scared of losing her mother to that mysterious force called death. She saw it in her mother's body, fixed, rigid, her serene reserve gone, face distorted to an ugly shape; she peered through the slits in the swollen flesh of eyelids. Little details, which would stay with her, like how Mother's skin was grey as ash. Fingers plucking at the quilt's edge. The blood stains down the front of her dress. Her brother remained paralysed and was of no help. "It was three men in uniform…three of them… three of them—" There was a smell of a different kind too. "They threw petrol on me— They were going to burn me… burn—" From that fateful day, till she died, Mother vibrated with a steady shudder.

The archaeology of childhood memories was not ordered in her adult mind. It was more like earth under a spade, turning up things forgotten, not simply memories but states of mind, emotion. She tried to cry out, as one does in a nightmare, but could make no sound, and she watched the past become her present.

⌘ CONTAMINATED ⌘

We don't have memories. Our slate remains bare as a grain of sugar. We cannot bottle memories, so, for Us, they slip away as warm days in winter, cold days in summer. But vessels like Her are different. They gather memories like twigs, thorns, and thistles and brambles.

Subjected to extreme physical savagery, a past so fixed got triggered, and as the flash of light followed by the thunder of pain fettered to Her as a corpse to a living person, the memory of that damned night resurrected itself. The ghosts of Her remembrances thronged as dead leaves whirling in autumn wind and She walked through it even though it was destructive, ugly and a source of pain.

We sensed Her in a trance, in the ridge and the swell and the surge and the rush of memories. That is when We got a chance to peek out. It was just for a moment, when there was a gap. Injected with some drug, She was too dull to stop Us. She seeped into a corner. It was Our chance to seep out. And for Her to sink in. She lost control, forgot about Us. She was in no condition to offer resistance to Us. The moment would not last, so We made the most of it.

When the men plundered Her body, She wasn't there anymore. There was only Us. They could not touch Us, no matter how hard they pushed into Her body.

We expanded against the walls, filling it up, blocking Her out completely. She wasn't even a small thing curled up in the corner of

Her head. We drained him. By the time he left the room crying, We were already riding him. Guzzling him. His energy was a sticky fruit sliding between our fingers and, when We were done, We were still hungry. The image of the man holding his torn finger in his hand, his nail tearing through his flesh and ligament, and his screams at the blood bursting, stayed with us. Blood. And We wanted more.

Blood drops smeared Her face and body, making Her shine with terrible beauty. When the manacles rattled on Her wrist and She was struck with blows, We could have made sure She did not feel a lash. But She did not seek Us out.

No Frenzy comes unsummoned. No Frenzy comes unbidden. We were hungry inside Her, raging against the useless mortality We were saddled with. It was an insult to be subject to the decisions made by what was just a vessel. To be carried as cargo. To be used, abused, punctured, fucked. We prodded Her. Strange waking dreams gripped Her. We filled Her with visions. And they never came alone. They dragged other things along. She knew they were coming from inside Her. And, that, to destroy them, they would have to destroy Her. She carried a world of dead souls inside Her.

We had tasted Blood. Now, all We needed was Her belief. Blood and Belief. It had started and It could not be reversed.

8

The seventh night of her confinement, Amba felt someone reach for her in the dark and tug at her hood. Motionless, she braced for the rape. The legs of her bed-plank scraped on cement as someone leaned over, and then, a hand yanked off the blindfold.

Who?

The man did not reach for her breast or place his hand inside her thigh. Instead, he placed a hand on her mouth.

"Shhhhhhhh! No noise! Get up. You are coming with me. Don't ask questions. Move it, girl—we don't have time!"

Two vertical lines, drawn by an invisible marker, creased her forehead as deft fingers peeled off her gag and untied her ropes. Her jawline was indigo and a sick green pulsed around her temples where she was hit; her eyebrows, so expressive, were held tight by anguish.

"But w-who are you?" Amba asked, but in reality, no legible words came out of her mouth. She croaked in pain and moistened her bleeding lips with the tip of her tongue. Every bone in her body ached and sores covered her feet. Her head swayed, nerves jolted into free-wheeling spasms and she tottered. Her vision was getting affected as patches of green mist floated before her eyes.

"Don't worry. My name is Nathan Ray. I am a government official. You are in no danger from me. Trust me, if you don't leave now, you are never getting out of here." Nathan said.

His voice was resonant as aged wood and Amba sensed he was an ally. For a moment, she saw herself suspended in determined black eyes; twin, flickering images. It was a rediscovery of self in a new space as seen by another.

"W-water...please...water...just want water..." she croaked in pain. And Nathan quickly gave her some water.

Even after quenching her thirst, moving an inch was more than she could manage. Exhausted, she leaned heavily against a reinforced concrete suspension. But it gave way under her weight. The inky sky added matter where there was none, and created the illusion of strength, which was absent. She would have fallen badly if Nathan had not quickly spun towards her and opened his strong arms to hold her. They moved forward, gingerly testing the floorboards with small, cautious steps. It was brutally cold and, under the bridge, crisp foam lay in a frost-grey film on the dark waters, bloated with enormous reeds.

She crumbled on her knees several times from the excruciating pain, and each time, Nathan gently held her, his arms strongly wrapped about her waist.

"If we try to escape from the front, a dozen guards will cut us down before we even reach the outer wall of the compound," Nathan said, casting a look over his shoulder for guards. "There is another way and that's all you have—shhhh!"

An unexpected noise caused her to freeze in the dark shade of the giant old barricade, with ice crawling up her skin. The low moan became a snarl.

It was Whip. Without any warning, he closed in on her. Her reflexes held good and she moved back to escape his outstretched grasp. She jerked an elbow into his stomach and heard the breath escape his mouth with a deep groan. All of a sudden, it seemed she had lost control of herself; and she drew a breath from deep inside her and blew on his face.

Whip's eyes were muddy and uncomprehending.

"You—! How did you come out, witch—" he started to say, but did not finish.

He found it impossible to slow the speed of the blow that felled him in the head. Shower of gravel. Wind-milling arms. An extended hand that clawed at several branches and missed, and his head disappeared under the black waters. On his way down into the ravine, Whip's ribcage cracked as it hit the sharp, jagged rocks. She stepped away, not wanting to know that his nose ballooned from his face, and his legs—which ended in the interrogatory boots, the marks of which were still imprinted on her back—shrivelled like a fly sucked by a spider. She heard the sound of flesh rupturing wetly and the pops of breaking bones. A group of startled crows exploded from the under-bush, cawing indignantly against the sudden disruption.

Whip's death was quick and painful. A flash by, with the swift, deceptive ease of an accident. She stepped back from the edge, thinking how horrible it was the way his body bent when it struck the surface of the water—a grotesque slapping sound of ripping tissue off the bones of his limbs. He was 'too drunk', they would say the next day.

"The rest of the guards will be here any moment. There is no way out. They will catch us and then no one can save me from them," Amba's voice was heavy with dejection. She leaned her weight on him and her body baulked with pain.

"There is a way out," Nathan said, hauling her upright.

He handed over his torch and the rifle and pushed her towards a gloomy black tunnel, hidden behind overgrown mouldy weeds, blackened with filth. The tunnel had been used as an escape route by anyone who knew it was there; from soldiers in olden times to freedom fighters and rebels and militants and, lately, criminals and all sorts of no-gooders and four-flushers.

"Good that I remembered about this discarded sewage tunnel from my last visit."

As he spoke, the muffled sounds of the change of guard filled the air, which meant there was no time to waste.

"The guards will be here any second—Go! The tunnel will take you to the forest. Don't look back! I will keep them distracted for as long as possible," Nathan said, before he disappeared towards the sound of the guards.

Amba gathered what remained of her strength and crouched to get inside the waste passage. The urgency to make distance from Baikaal was high and the sewage-filled bog was her passage to freedom. Some of the rotting innards, maggoty wood, fell flat upon the ground, rest quivered and trembled at every step. The tunnel reeked of the jail's smell—a mix of ammonia, battleship paint, sound deadening panels, electricity coursing through the security wires, singed flesh, burnt food, metal water and shit—a sorry, sodden stink of decay. Desiccated shrubs, strewn with garbage bags and broken plastic bottles, crunched under her feet; magazines rattled in the ammunition pouch around her waist. Amba teared up and gagged and, summoning up all her strength, huddled tightly and scrambled through the underground tunnel. It was bored in several places as a mining pipe, but all openings were plugged with fallen debris. She moved slowly and tentatively towards the nearest wall and slid her hands along the slick ridges. The dark soil was decanted of any pretence of life and was clogged with ancient residue. The air hung wet and low, and it hissed and whistled different songs, and near the exit, rumbled out a dark tune before it went hush.

The Jotsoma forest opened inwards into itself—abysmal and continuous, blackness onto blackness. She exited into a land not listed in any map, and such was its confusing geography that she ended up retracing her path several times. Her feet were covered with thorny brambles and lint and were green with moss. She ran till the cold froze her head and made her see double; she did not stop even when her shadow showed up in the morning haze and got long, so long that it extended to the other end of the mountain and disappeared altogether. She stood there, simply staring at the gaze-less trees, trying to soak in the sweet ethers, inhaling deep the incense fragrances, rubbing the special dust of the soil all over her body to get rid of the putrid smells of Baikaal. To some people, the Jotsoma was a strange, fearsome place. Moving in it a nightmare, and most would be ready to classify it as impenetrable. To Amba, however, the Jotsoma appeared only as a welcome means of concealed manoeuvre and surprise. And though she could not see due to the hour of the day, she must have been running through the marsh part. She knew from the sound of her breath; caustic, stale air scoured her lungs. She panted with the rhythm of the heavy rifle bouncing against her chest.

The mist was thick as milk, now; so that instead of her running at everything, everything seemed to run at her. Flakes fell on the trees, dazzling white, fine as a moth's wing and weightless. They caught in her hair, the moonbeams making each dark curl seem as though it was pulsating with a mysterious light. Her skin was illuminated by the stars, though she was deathly pale. She felt her heart would stop any moment and her brain started to defocus from the cold. Perhaps her ears had fallen off, for she could not feel them anymore. The air tasted less of burning sulphur, cordite, and the smell of pine got stronger, and she knew she was entering the unvisited and dangerous part of the forest.

9

At night, the Jotsoma transformed into a lethal playground of creatures from the bottom of some inferno frozen over. The night sky awakened predatory creatures and bloodcurdling howls heralded nameless terrors. Amba still did not have the knack of walking over brambles untouched, feeling her way over roots uncut, confused between a shadow and a sinkhole. Half-crazed with hunger, she knocked over a porcupine out of a tree and killed it with great tenderness and singed the quills into its flesh so she could get the benefits of every part. This was exactly the kind of hunger she had felt when, as a child, Mother served one quarter of a meal to her and gave three quarters to Nakul, saying boys needed more food. She was never angry with Mother, who would herself go hungry for days. The children always got their one-fourth and three-fourth.

A frozen swamp, full of black scales, spread out in front of her. Cautiously, she walked on the bog tufts, avoiding the frozen, oily mire. The cold rubbed off her vision and she stumbled and fell more than she ran. She kept checking for prowling footprints and slithering marks and gouges clawed in nearby trunks, and felt foolish. Until that moment, she did not know the number of things she feared. She entered a cave to escape the cold. The air inside smelled of a cemetery; it reeked of an alternate history monomaniacal yet directionless. The time-worn rocks and ancient trees, accumulated over ages, seemed to have conspired to create strange vegetation, bloated with oxblood squares of wrecked ground, broken acres of torn root, and drying pine needles strewn on tracts of reindeer moss and blades of flint. She was an earthworm, entering giant, untidy mounds of earth. She pushed through the thick air. The mist came fast and sudden. It closed in heavy, obscuring the cliffs, the sky itself and, within seconds, every bit of her exposed skin was slick with icy spray and that's when she saw them.

The dead bodies just lay there. Three men. Frozen grey. The corpses were seated with their backs stratified on the tree trunks. Their eyes were a dull hue, like a dead fish, the open mouths had changed to an ugly yellow. Over their grey faces ran little red ants, militantly trundling little bundles of their dead insides along their upper lip, all the way down to the ground to their nest in a determined thick line. She avoided moving near the dead bodies. Mother used to say that the spirits of the dead hang about their bodies, and noise, she thought, violated the dead at a deep level. The dead were dead, she told herself as practicality took over. None of them were coming back. Controlling the urge to retch, she said a quick prayer and retrieved the stiffened jacket wrapped around the smallest corpse. A small animal must have scraped against some rock—a small sound. She flinched. In a whirl of panic, she looked about for a place to hide. The noise turned out to be a false alarm. She wrapped the jacket tightly around herself and found a pitted ribcage of rotting hay, blocked with wild nettle and rubble. If nothing else, it would keep wild animals at bay during the night. Cold, hungry and exhausted, she slept for some time and dreamt of men chasing her, anticipating her every move, and her head spun from fear and thirst. Each breath triggered a rush of pain in her chest.

She woke in a few hours, her stomach growling. Weak from hunger, she waded into the nearby stream with plenteous silver fish. The icy water slowly climbed to her thighs and then her stomach and every second felt unendurable. Her rest and food-deprived body was ready to give in. The sand in the water was black and full of slippery weed. She planted her exhausted legs in the bed, fighting to stay afloat. Her wet clothes dragged her down, and her arms and legs felt heavy, as if made of iron. Finally, her eyes shut and her cramped arms could do no more, and just when she was about to let go, a plump silver fish jumped right into her hands. She devoured it raw and dreamt of spicy eggs, pounds of rice cakes with chicken and mutton, and baby maguey cobs fried in butter. A dipping mist almost covered the pit and, hungrier than ever from all the struggle, she ate another fish, unheeding of the icy rain lashing at her. She followed the trail cut through the burdock ragweed and pokeweed, and felt the poisonous poke berries smash against her arms and face, to arrive at a pigpen built of old iron and wood cement forms wired together. As the pig shit smells hit her, she saw the dim outline of a skinny dark hog up to its belly in mud. She switched on her flashlight. The swampy twelve-by-twelve-foot pen didn't show a sign of life in its soupy muck.

It was only when she started losing feeling in her extremities, when her eyelids were laden with ice, when she lost all thoughts except to take that next step, when sections started shutting off one after the other, did she realise the imminent danger of losing more than her extremities. She had to find a warmer place to take shelter. Soon. The temperature continued to drop, the wind got harsher and attained a retina-numbing quality, stripping every vestige of feeling.

It began as a low-pitched growl.

Of some beast close on her heel. Closer and closer and still closer. Fear sloshed her, each wave colder than the last, and she stepped back and was immersed in a sudden cloud of rancid air from an underground stream. She gagged. The sound grew hollow and echoed off the stone walls of the cave.

In a moment of fast-beating incomprehension, she was staring right at it. The dark seemed to step forward and the sound of her heartbeat now filled the forest. Like an apparition from her nightmares, the creature revealed itself and stood towering over Amba. From that moment, the universe had only two creatures.

Beast.

Her.

She trembled as one does when one sees, in real life, the stuff of nightmares, staring back with phosphorescent, disembodied eyes, straight out of the myths of a *Habishi* lore—a monster buffalo.

It took a threatening step. Its fiery eyes pinned her to the ground. Skin glistening dark as the bowels of the Hori mountain, the beast's size was made larger by the pitch black it was silhouetted with. Enormous horns added to the beast's height, its mighty hooves borrowed from some prehistoric creature. Every muscle focused in her direction, it bellowed loud, preparing itself for battle. A strangled growl escaped her. She did not want to die here and she definitely did not want her flesh to end up in the stomachs of monstrosities roaming in the jungles of the Jotsoma.

The beast let out a wail. It was the sound of piercing chaos. Amba discovered scorching fear. Beard flipping in the air, drivelling from its mouth, the beast charged with a roar towards her. Eyes, till now dead holes stuck in corpulent grey flesh, flashed with sparks of orange fire. The beast limped and shivered and glared and growled; and its teeth chattered in its head as it almost seized her by the chin.

It came roaring and resentful; but in the very centre of the clearing, its growls were suddenly hushed and she saw its great head lower and flatten out, the body crouch, and the long tail quiver with menace.

Let loose from the great dark, the beast rushed, bounding and roaring towards her. Too weak to fight back, she knew it was the end. But, without any warning, the beast stopped dead in its tracks. It opened its mouth and bellowed and the noise set her hair on end.

Then, the unthinkable happened.

⌘ BLOOD, BELIEF, SACRIFICE ⌘

The Buffalo-Shaman recognised Us inside Her. It identified Us under Her skin, smelled Us in the air that weaved itself around Her. It spoke to Us in its spirit tongue. A many-layered voice, like metal tearing through air, the Buffalo-Shaman's voice pounded the ground with its vibration. Language is only a human thing. There are other ways to talk. Which never seem stunted by lack of knowledge or awkward expression. That slip from the tongue and taste correct.

"Do you hear Us?"

We asked the Buffalo-Shaman. It replied in its spirit-tongue that carried as a whistle-song in the air.

"I hear all your voices, speak as One."

The Buffalo-Shaman addressed both Her and Us. We could feel Her shock when She first heard the Buffalo-Shaman through Us. At the sound of its voice, somewhere deep within Her, deeper than the ash of Her bones, eyes tore open. We felt One—the shaman and She and Us—together, balanced for a brief velvet moment.

"We are tired and hungry and cold, and will not last a night in this form in this forest."

"Perhaps now you won't be anymore. You have been waiting for me. I was waiting for you too to shed my skin and be finally free."

The Buffalo-Shaman said what it had to say. We knew what that meant. It was a sacrifice. The Buffalo-Shaman was offering its life to save Hers.

"In the forest, your laws don't work. To survive, you must obey me, surrender to my command. I allow you to shelter in my body. Heed my command. I give you permission to feed on me, on my blood and flesh."

"We don't want to kill you, for you have lived by wit and courage."

"When you have rested in me as a child, it will make me a mother again. I am clean of birth fluids now, and dry. I am half-way into the dark anyway. The longer I live without it bringing colour to my world, the more I love darkness. From this dark pit, others call out to me. I have no wish to be lonely."

The Buffalo-Shaman had spoken its will. We conveyed it to Her. But We could sense Her hesitation. We prodded Her repeatedly, "We will help You with the weapon. We will put the weapon in Your hand and remove the conscience from Your mind."

We pressed on Her. She balked. We nudged Her again, "There is no right and wrong. Only what You can and cannot do. Let Us close the door behind You."

We pushed Her till She held the weapon. There was learning for Us, too—blood and belief needed sacrifice.

10

The beast's lips moved and out came a strange voice—a half-whistle, half a song. A warning and a yearning. The sound of strange murmurings and creakings, of wild hollows swelling in the dark. A nameless language. As it rang out, strange birds began to scream and Amba's hair stood on end, thinking of the twisty trunks shivering like limbs of yet unseen monsters. Between the raspy cough that followed each torturous breath, it raised its vast wrinkled forehead into the sky, its hooves some twenty or more feet into the air, and bellowed. The air around it shivered with spray of clammy mud from its fur; she wondered what the beast thought and what it saw. Snow, pine needles, trees, smoke, blood—she shuddered.

The noise rose and swelled—louder than a village of storms—with all their confluent waves, dazzlingly broke against the air tossing and spraying in the air, and what she heard seemed soaked in water and smothered in mud and lamed by stones and cut by flints and stung by nettles and torn by briars. The beast snuffled forward, its nose working. Haunted eyes stared out from a ghost of bones and sinews. It was merely ten feet away. She could see the creature, a female, was mainly a hide draped loosely over rickety bones. The hot furnace roar of its breath was now upon her. Amba's face felt dry and grimy and crackled with every breath. She knew what she had to do. Though she felt the world was being cordoned off into the spectator section, in her head she experienced no loss of awareness. In its brown eyes, there was a depth of sorrow that shook Amba even in her desperation; for despite her anguish, she had to do the unthinkable to save her own life. It was only when she aligned with the voices inside her that an unmooring of all her functions started making more sense than anything in the world. Amba emptied her mind with the strength of her will and became very still. She thought of exactly nothing at all. Her hands shook and her legs kept giving out. Her vision was getting cloudy from the cold and her lips had turned to ice. She was losing all feeling in her fingers. Then the snow came down and she knew there was no time.

She bowed before the beast's beating heart and felt the connection to the distension and contraction of its organs. The beast moved in such a way as if to nudge her to aim with her gun, point at its heart, and fire. A sacrifice offered such, broke her heart, but she fired the gun. The bullet hit the beast with a sickening thud as metal pierced flesh and it wasn't enough. She was jolted by the report of the rifle; the bullet striking the bowlder behind its body; startled, as if it was not her hand which did it. Several more bullets found their mark before the beast crumbled lifeless and still. She fell beside it, wracked with grief. A great rift opened in her heart. A crack so deep, it went down forever. Amba plunged her knife into the beast's underbelly to put it out of its misery. Tears streaming down her face, she chewed on raw slices of liver and heart. A fragrant stream in the blood stirred her to life and she worked, quickly wrenching away the guts, cleaning out the rib cavity.

Overwhelmed by her act and overcome by grief, she fell into a faint, exhausted and drained. By now, almost dead with exertion and cold, she snuggled close to the carcass and stayed in the position for an hour, where she crept close to death. Butterflies whirred. Fluttered. Rained. So many of them. She choked. She could not breathe. They were in her hair, in her ears, eyes. They felt heavier and smelled metallic. Like moths. Hundreds of them. Coming from some hole, attracted to the smell of her. She shook her head left and right and up and down. Hundreds of moths whirred about. Settled back. They were not moths, but little flies attracted to the hot blood. Overcome with revulsion, she shook her head crazedly. They settled back. The knife cut into the beast's soft underbelly and she crawled inside. She swooned into a dead sleep with the sudden comfort, a full belly and the golden warmth pressing on her. The mind started slipping. She imagined herself in the belly of the whale—entangled in the deep muck of deceptions, a dark womb.

Desperately, she tried to get a hold on the slimy tissue. The slippery slopes pushed her down to a deeper, darker black. The tissue broke when she pushed too hard and she fell into a secret box buried in a quicksand, with locks and fetters and suddenly set free. Thoughts slid in and she caught her breath; a traumatised child, who stumbled, having forgotten the faces of those she held dear. A collage of faces, maddening, confusing, burst in her head—a collection of constantly changing shapes and sizes and skin, hair, eyes and lips and clothes, dimensional blobs of pulsating everything. It was dangerous to get inside a buffalo even in a deadly storm, everyone knew that. Yet, in Her delirium and drawn to its warmth, she crawled into the carcass, which was so warm, a primeval womb.

Once inside its body, she became the buffalo.

The buffalo adopted her.

She was buried alive in a cage of the buffalo's red blood and guts and bones.

Amba knew, with every pore of her being, there was no going back. The present and the future were lost to her forever, of that she was sure. She awoke choking. Frantic from loss of air, she dragged her rifle and kept it at a point and managed to blast herself an air hole. Fresh air gushed into her lungs. Amba's eyes broke the top of the thick frozen tissue and quietly surveyed the scene to get a sense of her position. Poking the barrel outside the hole, to keep from freezing over, she waited for the sun to come out. She studied the wall with stains, she saw fantastic landscapes and strange rivers and flying rocks and trees and plains and valleys and hills, figures in battle with strange faces and objects, and the patched and peeling surface, roughened and stained with grime and damp and its accidental shapes and colours. It became strangely interesting to look at, the process of decay having created a pattern in which one sees a natural drama in progress of life, trying to keep imminent death at bay.

Her movements caused disturbances in the forest air that could be easily smelled by predators. She was going to have to remain submerged as much as possible to minimise the ripples and eddies from her body. A few slow inhales and exhales later, she sank under the skin and tissue, while keeping her left hand on the wall of the culverts so the body's current wouldn't move her. She willed her body into an extreme relaxed state. The danger was that it was possible to float out from, because it was so squishy inside if she got too comfortable. The blood was still warm and so was she. But not for long. Over time, her body would lose heat to the point of hypothermia. Drifting into sleep could be fatal and she kept biting her lips, and wiggled her head into the air pocket.

Disoriented, she dreamt she was stuck upside down in the flesh and slowly drowning—one long, unbroken nightmare of hideousness—that she soon lost all track of time. She imagined Mother and Father, coated from hair to boot in dirt and blood, falling into a crevice, while she tried to get them out. Then everything erupted to life and started exploding around them and she slipped and fell inside on top of them and they went past the blast walls, cracked from different explosions, and sewage-laden goop, then sank further down, and she inhaled its bitter, burning viscous blood. Instead of waking up, she plunged headlong into another nightmare. Serpents for hair, scorpion tails and eyes dripping blood, the demon accosted her. Grey, pitiless face, cut from living blood. She almost imagined a forked tongue flicking from his lips. Dark wings stuck to her back and demonic tails swished behind her and weaved living ribbons and waves through her hair. She imagined thin, green worm snakes and whip in her hand, its tip rasping faintly as she dragged it through the floor, and the still sane part of her mind was shocked at what it was witnessing. Time became a living entity, a pre-historic whale, and she, stuck inside a giant stomach, watching the seconds, minutes and hours that passed, never to return, marking her forever with their imprint, elastic enough to stretch some moments to eternity and brittle enough to dissolve entire years into vapour.

She woke up struggling frantically for breath. Hitting out right and left with her arms and legs, at last something gave way, and she found her nose surfacing in the fresh air. The blood draping her body had solidified to stone and she wondered if this was how she was meant to die. There was no pain as she floated on top, looking down at herself, drowning in blood, even though she managed to get her head slightly out. The rest of her was slowly freezing to death inside the beast, even as all around them, thick mist draped over the river, pale as flesh of a phantom.

Faint outlines of a figure emerged from the mist.

For a few initial moments, Amba assumed it to be some phantasm, a part of the procession of nightmares. But then, the figure crouched over her, holding the unmistakable outlines of a large dagger, and when foreign air invaded her lungs—dense, heavy and cold—she realised it was no dream but happening for real. A smell, familiar as her own skin, of earth and clinging roots, salt iron and blood, cordite and sulphur engulfed her. A sudden rush of comprehension discharged the last crumbs of sanity and the walls of blackness crashed on her from all sides. With half-frozen eyes, she glimpsed the small-sized figure slowly approach her through the fog, on what appeared to be cloven hooves.

11

As long as he could remember, he was planning to kill somebody. Rosie Madbull revelled in the process of killing. Just about anything could be a trigger. Things people wouldn't even notice. Things people just let pass. Not him. Not the mental ledger in his head.

"You see the enjoyment that's always underrated, the joy of killing," he would often say after a kill.

His preoccupation with death could have begun years ago when his father was killed in front of him. Lynched by a tribal mob because he beat one of the factory workers to death. Mr Madbull had got enraged because the worker, an indigenous tribesman, had the gall to demand an increase in wage. The killing was supposed to be a warning to others harbouring similar ideas. Unluckily for Mr Madbull, the sequence of events did not quite play out the way he imagined. The same day, while returning from the market with twelve-year-old Rosie, a group of tribal boys caught hold of them and dragged the father–son duo to a pre-determined place.

'The scaffold must have been built in a hurry', was Rosie's first thought when he saw it. Rosie was made to watch as the hangman tested several ropes to hang his father and kept one for backup. No one physically harmed Rosie, he was a mere boy, after all, harmless. They couldn't have known the little boy's mental ledger added it differently.

At the appointed hour, a huge crowd filled the field and beyond. Mr Madbull was taken on a horse-drawn wagon and made to sit on a pile of unburnt wood—to be his pyre soon, Rosie was told. When he saw his father lying almost dead, he felt no tenderness for him, just an impatience and contempt and the question, *'why doesn't he just get up?'*, which he would have asked if he could. Rosie did not stick around for the hanging and walked all the way home, his shirt drenched in his father's blood. The smell of blood never left his nostrils. He grew to savour it.

That day, Madbull learned things about blood. That it was messy when it was made to leave the confines of the veins which held it. Inside, it ran clean in tiny tubes that split and branched into millions of tributaries, an ancient ocean system. Inside, it did not stray, or lose any essential amount of itself while all five litres of it finished the nineteen-thousand-kilometre long and laborious journey every day, day after day. Outside the confines, it was out of control. He learned that blood dried. Divided. Cracked. Stank. Died. Became useless when out of its confines. Blood should stay in its pre-determined place if it has to stay alive.

In Baikaal, he and only he had the *power* to control which and how much blood would remain in its confines. Amba's daring escape was an act of ultimate provocation, which had damaged the arrangement. It had shifted the power equation. He had been made to look like a fool by the girl. The roaring anger beneath his skin was getting difficult to control. But first, there were the loose ends to be dealt with.

"She picked grenades by hand and nothing happened?" Madbull said with the demeanour of a man whose cruelty sprung fast as weed.

"Yes, Colonel. One by one. Like she was picking eggs," the guard replied.

"This man, you say, saw it with his own eyes?"

"Yes. Absolutely."

"What do they think of her in the village?"

"A troublemaker. People are scared of her, keep out of her way."

"But a witch? If that was so, then why did she not cast a spell, turn all to stone, reduce the jail to ash with a curse? A strange *witch* she is who allows herself to get caught, gets beaten and spoiled repeatedly and yet does not let out a peep."

"Maybe she was enjoying it."

At that, everyone started laughing. All, except Mathera, who looked pensive.

"She will return." The tittering faded into silence. "All witches take their revenge," murmured someone else.

"I got a good look. She was no witch," said a guard with authority.

"Witch or not, there is no way she would have survived in the jungle. There are bloodthirsty beasts of the type we cannot imagine...!" replied his companion in hushed tones.

"I don't care which lowlife, slave-holder, four-flusher devil's hole this so-called witch is hiding in...Get her back to Baikaal."

Madbull's voice held the thrum and charge of low military drums.

"Yes, Colonel."

"She will wish she was dead," promised Mathera. He said like a man with an unslaked appetite for fights, uglier the better.

"What a strong animal, though! That she could stand after the boys having a go at her all night."

"A decent woman would have died of pain if not the shame of it. Filthy animal," Mathera said.

"They are all animals. Nothing decent about them. They are subhuman. That's why we need to get rid of them and let civilisation in."

"If the stories of a witch running around in the Jotsoma spreads, I don't see prospectors lining up for the license. That's the end of the good life."

"No man can do business if there are so many witches running about!"

"Bad for business. No man can do business with some witch's curses to worry about!"

"By god, we hunt them down. That's what we do."

That Madbull spent the last few years deploying his entrepreneur skill, building a commercially successful contractorship, and now his efforts stood threatened by a girl, a *Habishi* no less, was intolerable. Like his father, Rosie Madbull too, regarded all tribals as nothing more than beasts, their women unknowable, their customs fearsome and primitive, their resistance—unexplainable. What else could explain the fact that despite the continued embargo, resulting in drying of supplies and extreme shortage of necessities, not one villager was ready to leave his land? This defiance was an open challenge to him, and the loss of business was an unpardonable offense. To a man like Madbull, the loss of good revenue was the ultimate provocation.

"A fucking chit of a girl managed to shove her tail between your fucking eyes. And she sits right now, flaunting herself and boasting about how she fooled Madbull. Tell me, what part of that do you think is right?"

The guard's lips curled malignantly, cringing under an expected blow. Madbull watched him squalling in his fear, and, like any bully, the fear he glimpsed in the weaker man seemed to cheer him up inordinately.

"I asked a question. I order you to answer me."

"It will not happen, Colonel."

"I hate cock and fuck coming out of your mouth."

"Sorry, Colonel."

"In combat, destruction of the enemy is the only objective. If you fail in that, you are a burden. You have to take responsibility of your act."

"Yes, sir. Someone has to be responsible."

"How many guards were on duty the night the witch escaped?"

"Two."

"We have found the remains of one who obviously put a valiant fight when the witch tried to escape and was martyred. Who was the second guard?"

Silence.

"I don't repeat myself."

"Me, Colonel. It was me." A greenish pallor enveloped the guard and he took the colour of a malarial patient.

"Louder. Who would that someone be?" Madbull asked; seething anger crouched inside him.

"Colonel, I had fever. The chief guard granted me leave from duty."

"That's true, Colonel," Mathera replied.

"Duty. That's the bottom line. Someone is always responsible when there is a lapse. Someone irresponsible would be a loose end."

"Yes, Colonel."

The thin lips drew back tightly against yellow teeth in a grimace that was nothing but hideous. The rage was vast when it came. Madbull moved with lightning speed, knocked the man forward and fired point-blank. A sickening thud-plop, the sound of metal tearing through flesh rang through the silence. With a livid face Madbull stood, leaning for support against the table; his knees shaking in anger beneath his bulky carcass; while his lips were drawn apart against his yellow teeth in a grimace.

"Drown the fucker in diesel to preserve his body and we will pack the corpse in epoxy—make a paperweight out of him or something. Or better still, just throw him into the gorge behind Baikaal." The men silently obeyed the Colonel's orders, careful not to antagonise him further.

"Gentlemen—there is always someone responsible," Madbull said, instantly good-natured and affable. A man of refinement. Not someone who just shot another man at point-blank range. Smiling amiably, he requested for tea to be delivered to the special cell in the basement. No one seemed to notice the dead body which lay in a widening pool of dark blood.

Rosie Madbull had another appointment and he did not want to be late for it.

Nathan looked diminished, having spent the most of the day locked in the cold cell he had been asked by Madbull to inspect. All his attempts to pry open the basement cell door had come to a nought, for there was simply no handle or mechanism to grab. He had run his hands along the metal umpteen times without any purchase. It was strange to reach for the door and find nothing to grasp. A part of him knew it was no accident. He was being held in custody.

"Let me out, Madbull," he shouted the moment he saw the Colonel walk in.

Madbull looked at him from across the room but made no move to help. Instead, he dragged a chair and sat down looking at him with compassion from the other side of his prison cell's iron gate. Pale, red light of the dying day fell slantwise across Madbull and froze the eddies of smoke about him, fixing each coiling thread with menace and a sinister meaning.

"Would you like some tea?"

Madbull spoke, as if talking to a friend and not to an adversary he had confined against his will. In his massive hands, the china cup seemed impossibly fragile; he might anytime choose to close his fist and, with a single motion, crush the vessel to dust; a jungle cat tapping a small bird back and forth with the flat of its paws.

"Tea? Are you mad? Let me out, you psycho—"

"I will not do that, so no need to be vulgar."

"How long do you plan to hold me?"

"See, here is the thing. You come with a gun to my bar, things will happen. Unpleasant things will be set in motion. So, don't you complain if you get a face full of pellets. You remember that you are the one that got the gun into my bar first. Just that I have a better gun, and a better aim."

"You cannot keep me here forever!"

"Mr Nathan, you continue to surprise and annoy me. It could have been so cordial—you should have left with your evidence file, your damn complaint, no one was stopping you! But you *had* to poke your nose into my business—you ask questions about Madbull's private army, you get too nosy and you think it won't get back to me? And what good did it do for you? See where it landed you."

"So you *do* have a private army? I am told the worst brutes populate this secret band of men? What foul business do you have them do?"

"Your suggestion is both accusatory and inaccurate." He twitched his gun to emphasise the point. "But imagine, you going back and spreading panic just before prospector season starts? That cannot be allowed."

"Are you saying that I will remain a prisoner? Under what charges?"

"Let's not be coarse. We will just establish the routine questions. You were locked up for your own safety. Can you imagine if the locals—the barbaric *Habishis*—got their hands on you, a government representative at that, what they would do!"

"You are a lunatic."

"Lunatic! *Am* I? Mr Nathan, I am the one who will rid the land of the taint—the vermin of *Habishis*, the termites, for good."

"All this for what? Just for the gold in their land?"

"Just for the gold? Tell that to the wild projectors who seek to heap up gold by the bushel and the cartload, instead of scraping it together, coin by coin. Do you know what kind of money we are looking at? Prospectors have flooded the township, swelled the population and filled the hotels in the valley down below to capacity. Everyone wants an in, everyone wants to pull an old favour and get a license to put a spade to Hori mountain's chest. Offices to settle claims, mining rights and brokers with pledges, orders from rich men, are being set up in the valley right now, surely you know—this place would be a hive of industry; it is changing forever."

"They will have no stake, no compensation, and no one will even ask these poor people what they want."

"What do you imagine we are? We are not the band-aids on their giant sucking chest wounds! We—WE are the guns. Are you even listening? You can have a stake in this, too! How long before they retire you with a little pension and you finishing your days, rotting in some old age home? You can be part of this. Every hour, a new frame is being hammered into place, new stores unfurling their banners to crack in the wind. The metal itself, hidden in the hills, whose aggregate value was so colossal, it had not yet been added up. It's mind boggling! You think this should be left to the barbarians?"

"And to damn with the *Habishis*? To hell with their rights?"

"Their *rights*? We are not exactly dealing with respectable people, having grand cultural traditions. Barbarians don't have rights in a civilised society. Join hands with me. C'mon, Mr Ray, you and me are very alike."

"I am not like you in any way, you lunatic, and you will never get permission to drive them out."

"Permission? That is just an annoyance, only the minutest annoyance, the merest flyspeck in a five-gallon pot of cocaine—because in this fucking shitty town, I am king. I am god. I will do as I please."

Madbull thoughtfully turned his hands over, studied the whorls on the pads of his fingers and appeared to tally his losses. He began speaking in a style that was almost poetically exaggerated and accented by proverbs, the meaning of the words uttered seemed profound, but not particularly clear. He said, "A man with no memory is a man with no foresight." And "Any man who held a gun with both hands was a fool" and "A big tree always has dead branches." The comments lacked any immediate context and Nathan was at his wits end as he realised Madbull's descent into psychopathic paranoia was final. And that made him not responsible for his actions and much more dangerous.

"I have to report back, and if I don't, enquiries will be made," Nathan said, knowing well the words were lost on the psychopath.

"You have met Mathera? You must have seen him around. On the offside, doesn't he look the sort of man who would get pleasure from sticking hands in the barbarians' slimy, pink viscera, examine their flaccid dicks and feed to the dogs their putrefying scrambled eggs of their brains? He will, too. Allow me to finish. Mathera, it turned out, has a brother in the department—"

"What a coincidence!"

"Only a weak mind puts faith in coincidence. Mathera here tells me no one is aware of your presence here. It seems, no one will know where to look if, at all, they miss you. And even if someone thinks of looking here, the locals are uncontrollable in their rage and took it out on the government functionary, so Colonel Madbull and his regiment will not be held responsible!"

Madbull lowered himself to his knees and looked through the muck tray slot. He reached through the opening and extended the ring of master keys.

"Should we write a letter, Mr Nathan Ray? To the General, on your behalf? You will apprise him of the danger the *Habishis* pose and how they have attacked you."

"I will write no such thing."

"You don't have to write anything. I have done most of the drafts. All that is missing is your seal."

"No one will believe the lies!"

"They will, for some time. You underestimate the stupidity of government officials. Besides, truth is not a matter of fact. It's a matter of consensus."

He was now a war veteran. Respectable and grand. Then again, he was a creature of death. And malevolence. A pale-eyed psychopath, at home with ruffians, and murderous, sulky and fractious.

"And if you want to know the secret—it is simple. If you want a well-behaved Red-Hound, you just have to do one thing. Give them an opportunity to kill things. Kill as much as possible. Murder sorts them out," Madbull said like a general gazing upon a massacre he had ordered to satisfy a personal blood lust.

12

The *Habishi* women were desolate. For the last few days, the only milk their cows deigned to give was either bloody or reeked of unwholesome mucous. The village shaman's doomsday jabber added to the growing unease and everyone was wrapped in a pall of gloom. All except Tara. Because Coral was untouched by malaise; her milk glistened with vitality and got sweeter by the day. There was another reason for the spring in Tara's step.

Last night, Nakul had returned home earlier than expected and she was relieved to see him in a pleasant mood. She was careful not to bring up the topic of Tanu Bakar or Amba for fear of antagonising him. Instead, she spent hours pampering and loving him.

Soon it was obvious to her that Nakul did not seem to notice her efforts, so she tried harder and kissed him on his mouth but he looked almost repelled. As if the idea of love-making was suddenly obscene. Tara was gripped with doubts, and guilt. Doubts over what remained of his love for her, and guilt for having let him stack his bitterness like years of harvest. Because now it was rotting, and it reeked of anger and long memories and petty ways. And it was too late to set new rules. Nakul had always exhibited a selfishness that he seemed to think was his birth right. And because she loved him with all her heart, she always let him feel entitled to his grief. But now she was frightened, for both of them. He saw that and took her with extra passion, as if to make up for embarrassing her. She did not stop him, thinking if this was what it took to make him feel better, to make her husband remain with her for some more time, so be it.

Despite all the love they shared, his light seemed to grow dim and he looked benumbed by some crushing guilt. Nothing she said could compensate for the loss of that solid, inward comfort of mind, which comes easily to the guilt-free, nor could it fight the horror which the nameless shame introduced in his heart.

She did feel that she could trust him and she loved him, all the same, she could not look at him without an inward shudder. When it was over, he rolled away, without looking at her. She lay still, not wanting to move, not daring to move. They stayed like that and she felt tears running down the sides of her cheek, and didn't know if they were his or hers. She wrapped her arms around him and they both lay still.

"Is it true, what they say?" she asked softly.

"About what?"

"You know, what Madbull and the others claim, that there is gold under our soil."

"Whether or not there really is gold is not important. Madbull believes it is there. And there is not a soul in the world who can convince him otherwise."

"But how does he plan to get it?" she said with a shudder.

"From what I have heard about Madbull, he does not waste time thinking. He gets what he wants. And hell awaits those who come in his way."

"Won't the government stop him? I heard there was an inspector from outside to check on him. The state will protect us. They will not let anything to happen to us."

"You are too naïve. Anyone can be bought with the promise of gold. Madbull will be at it till we give up our land. I think he has started enjoying our desperation."

"What will become of us...will we lose our houses? Will he force us to move?" she asked.

"More wars. It leaves us with many more wars," Nakul said, before descending into a sullen silence. "This war is changing me," he said finally.

"I hope the war is over by the time the baby comes," she managed to say.

"War? Which war? I don't care," Nakul said, looking disoriented, and then added, "But I suppose there is always war—there always is."

"Are you feeling unwell? My god, you are sweating! You have fever...you should rest!"

"Help me, Tara. I feel I am in a demonic boat, sliding towards a waterfall. All of a sudden, a surge of water comes and carries me away from you," Nakul whimpered, his face flushed.

"I want to help you; there is nothing I want more! But if you don't tell me what plagues you, if I don't know the cause of your sorrow, I am helpless. I am afraid of it. Like a blight, this wretched sadness inside you has become a pestilence. I don't want it to cast its cursed shadow on our baby."

At her words, Nakul looked up with such anguish that she stopped mid-sentence and took his hand in her own and told him how much she loved him. She tried to stroke his leg with her hand but he pulled away, as though she was hurting him. A gust of wind lifted his curly locks and whipped them against his cheek and the lash brought a film of tears to his eyes. His mouth was slightly open and his lips made delicate, rippling movements, perhaps looking for words.

"Everyone knows. I can see it in their eyes. They know what I did."

"What did you do, Nakul?" Tara asked. She was used to Nakul's bouts of self-doubt and guilt. But even she was spooked by what he had just said.

"I am a coward. A coward. A coward, that's me! Will you stop loving me when you know my truth, Tara?"

Nakul rocked back and forth, refusing to be still, as if, in stillness, he would have to deal with his pain and his regrets. She could almost feel on her the weight of his unrefreshed, motionless stare, the stare of a man who lies unwinking in the dark, passive in the toils of disastrous thoughts.

"Nothing can be so bad that it can make me stop loving you."

"You are too innocent. You don't know what I did."

"Tell me, my love."

"I thought—I was sure—I would be happy, when they took away Amba. Yes. I saw the soldiers attack her in front of my eyes. I hid. Did nothing. I thought, finally rid of her, I will be at peace."

Nakul's voice was dull. Then, he sobbed in despair, which seemed to be turning his skin inside out. The dreadful emptiness in his eyes, and a hollow moaning in his voice, like that of one being led to execution.

"No one will blame you."

Tara managed to say, her face solemn in the shadows. He pressed her hands to his chest, to the hollows and hard bones, as if torment gnawed at his chest.

"The thought torments me...drives me mad! I saw Mother light the matchstick...She looked at me...I did not stop her... Remained frozen." He broke down, wailing. Tara put an arm around him, holding him close to her bosom as his back convulsed with grief.

"Shh...It cannot be held against you," Tara repeated, her voice soft.

"Their memories are in my head...I cannot escape...It's powerful..."

"What is powerful?"

"Regret," Nakul said, as if unsure of the meaning of the word.

"Regret is meaningless," she said.

His body was rigid; he seemed to have swallowed a stone.

"Don't you see, Tara? I should have saved Mother. She loved me the most—she loved me more than Amba."

Nakul's grief was terrifying to see for Tara and she covered her eyes.

"She burnt herself; I was there and I did nothing. I could have done something. Did I not kill them, then?"

"Who am I to judge? Nakul, who am I to judge anyone?"

"Amba never reacted. Never showed any emotion. She did not even cry. All my life, I wished it had happened to her instead. I resented that she was still alive—and I failed to protect her, too."

"Shh—"

"You see, I've always been jealous. Jealous of all they said she was. And all I would never be...feeble fibres would not stir and prod life to well over its boundaries—"

"Shh—"

"But it's too late now. Too late for anything."

"No one's fault. Birth, death—nothing is in our hands. God ordains it," Tara said.

"You know, you are right. It cannot be my fault. She is half a witch—who knows, maybe she made it happen?" Nakul asked shrilly.

And then there was no stopping him.

The dam broke within him and he talked and talked. He told her he wanted to be free. He wanted to be ferocious. All those elements of himself he had pushed away, his sexuality, his desires. And he told her about Tanu Bakar. Overwhelmed by his own confessions, he sobbed softly.

"There was a time in my life when I expected the world to be full of new things. And then came the day when I realised that is not how it will be for me. My life is full of holes; things that were there and then were not, and though I grew around and between the holes, I can still reach my hand out to where things were and feel that dead hard of the space where the memories are."

"I will pray to the gods to grant us peace," replied Tara.

Faced with this new understanding of her husband, Tara looked baffled, and self-loathing hit Nakul. His grief was so raw, and he put his head on her lap. Tara looked away. He noticed her drawing slightly back and was embarrassed.

Tara suddenly looked worn out. She feared the longest sleep could not grant her rest. In this state, they lay beside each other in silence, through the long hours of the night. As dawn broke, they lay intertwined, occupied by their private demons, watching the cottony flakes which fell into the waters outside the window, till the sun was low on the far fields. It had been sleeting all morning and now a blue mist hung in the air and dispersed in icy gusts. Before leaving, he kissed the baby kicking inside her stomach and made her promise to teach the child not to have any remorse.

"Remorse," he said with a wistful finality as he got up to leave, "...Remorse has terrible and lasting power. Our child should have none of it."

"Teach the baby yourself," she said wryly. Nakul smiled and bent his head to kiss her, but she drew back, suddenly angry.

"Why are you going back to Tanu Bakar? You have always hated him anyway. Now, I am telling you, don't go. Stay with me. And you've heard, too, that Amba has escaped Madbull's jail and his men are combing the forests, looking for her. If they find out about you—that you are her brother..."

"This is my battle too, Tara."

"Stay with me, with us—don't run away—!"

"Is that what you think I am doing? Running away? You, too, think I am a coward!"

"No! But what can be more important than your family?"

"I have to go. There are things which have to be sorted."

The undertone of his words frightened her and she withdrew from his profanity, which reeked of the accumulated bitterness of years. It was no longer just about the new enemies he might be making because of this bitterness. He seemed so aloof, as if he had decided that there was no bringing him back into the world he had forfeited.

The pain was more than Tara could handle and she moved away from him, clutching her stomach, and sobbing coolly, as if mentally she had already resigned herself to the fact that he was lost to her, and that she would be alone for the rest of her life.

13

The signs worsened. Village dogs' howls grew longer and set everyone's nerves on edge. Even the docile Iravati churned out putrid dead fish. The elders supported the shaman on the signs being the harbingers of doom, but none could correctly guess what they portended. They were to find out the horrific implications by the end of that night.

It began with a knock on the heavily fortified village gate, late that evening. Two men, who identified themselves as 'government officers', demanded to be let in. They informed Headman Phamdom Lama that the village was to be 'inspected', following an intel tip that an illegal arms factory was going to be set up.

"We are officers from the city," the taller of the two men asserted solemnly as he asked the village chief for his cooperation. "And we need to investigate the matter. Setting up an arms factory in the village premises is strictly against the law. Those found to be involved in any way with such a criminal act will stand accused of plotting against the state."

"There is no need for you to investigate. I am the village headman and you have my word. Only women and children and old men are here. There is nothing illegal happening in my village. Also, neither Tanu Bakar nor his men are here."

"Well, in that case, you should have no objection to the inspection."

After a lot of deliberation, and a great deal of reluctance, it was decided there could be no harm in letting the two men in, provided they proved their identity. Almost as if expecting such a demand, the two men promptly offered their identity cards, holding them with both hands, thumbs and forefingers gripping their corners. They held their cards just below their faces and peered over like eager schoolboys as Phamdom Lama put a finger on each card to scrutinise it, while using the other hand to caress the rifle slung across his chest. Finally, they were both let in.

Setting about their job earnestly, the men moved house to house, making a great show of checking and writing comments in their little notebooks. And following them was an excited babble of children, aping the men as they went about making enquiries.

They were taken aback when they saw Tara's beautiful white calf, shining with heavenly health. Tara instantly offered them Coral's sweet milk, perhaps also as an insurance against any misadventure.

"Delicious! This is sweet," praised the first officer, sounding genuinely surprised.

"No sugar too," added the second officer.

"Wait here, mister. I will pack you some butter I made from her milk."

"Butter?"

Tara nodded proudly. The officers consumed more milk, but refused the fragrant white butter she packed for them. They had to move on and 'finish their job', they said, avoiding her eyes, and Tara felt the first prick of misgivings.

Soon, there was a commotion; the village headman's grandsons were dashing down the streets, yelling.

"They are here—they are here!" shouted the elder one.

"Hiding! They are all hiding behind the grove," cried the younger boy.

"Who is here, boys?" asked an alarmed Phamdom.

"Hundreds of them! The regiment troops. They are hiding outside." The panic in the boys' voice was loud enough for all to hear above the river's roar.

"Come here, boy. Speak slowly, what did you see?" Phamdom Lama's voice was grave.

"Uniformed men..."

"...too many to count!"

"And they have weapons..."

"...lots and lots of weapons!"

"Are you sure, boys? Were they just marching on? Because then there is no need for this panic."

"No, no! They are coming here—they are, they are!"

As if on cue, someone thumped just then on the village gate, which was closed after the officers were let in, and a voice boomed on the microphone.—

"I am Lieutenant of the Hill Regiment. I have orders from my commander. Our platoon has surrounded this village. We have received information that criminal Tanu Bakar and his accomplices are hiding here. And that they are holding two of our inspection officers hostage. This is a very serious offence. Hand over our men and all members of that criminal gang immediately."

"This is a mistake. Tanu Bakar and his men are not here. And as for your officers, they came on their own accord to inspect our village. You can confirm it with them yourself! No one is holding them hostage," Phamdom Lama shouted back.

"Let us in. We need to inspect the village by the rule of law."

"No. I cannot permit you to enter. Your officers will be here any minute now and they will tell you the truth. The gates will not be opened for any more of you," Headman Lama insisted.

"There is no need for this defiance, old man!" Sushithal hissed and interrupted the old chief, "We know there is nothing here. But they have weapons. Why are you making them angrier?"

"You will do well to shut up, boy! Hard to believe you are Tanu Bakar's nephew."

"Mind your words, stupid old man."

"I don't have the will to fight with you," he told Sushithal, before turning to the regiment officer at the gate. "Lieutenant sir, I repeat that you have no business getting men and weapons at our door. We are protected by laws too, and the law says you cannot trespass without valid reason. Your officers insisted to be let in. It was they who claimed that they had orders to check our village for an illegal arms factory," Phamdom Lama said, but he might as well have been singing to a dead hog.

"Outright lies! There are no such orders. We demand that you open the gates!"

"You are the one speaking lies, and your men. I am sure now that your men trespassed into our village and hid their true motives," Phamdom Lama shouted back, losing his patience. "But we will get them here and have them tell you the truth!"

"Chief…Chief! The officers…They have disappeared!" Chief Phamdom's grandsons shouted excitedly.

"What do you mean 'disappeared'? How is that possible?"

"We are not sure, but we cannot find them!"

"Enough of this drama!" the Lieutenant spluttered. "You are putting yourself and the whole village, the women and the children, in a bad position. We repeat, NO orders were given to search the village for any arms factory. We, too, have witnesses who swear they saw the officers being led away by your men. You have no option. Let us in and lead us to them."

"This is pre-planned trickery—a pretext to enter our village!" Phamdom rued. They were trapped. But he decided to brazen it out. "We cannot…will not…let you in. We demand that you leave our land and never return. Leave now."

"I don't think you have understood! You are not in a position to demand. You don't have any option. Don't be foolish. We have orders. You have to cede immediately."

"Looks like we do have an option. We are talking, aren't we?"

"Who am I speaking with? Show me your face."

"No. But I will tell you who I am. I am the one who is preventing you from barging into our land."

"We found them, we found them! They were hiding in the storage, planting explosives!" said one of the villagers as he held the two officers by the scruff of their necks and brought them to the front. He also held a small tell-tale bag of explosives.

"Now we know who are the criminals here, Lieutenant! Your men, these bloody liars, dared to get explosives into my village! They are our prisoners now. And they will remain so till you withdraw your troops."

There was a brief silence outside the village gate before a new voice boomed on the microphone. It was Colonel Rosie Madbull.

"Headman Phamdom Lama, you speak to *me*, now—Colonel Madbull. So, you can see that the matter is quite serious! You seem to think you have a choice in the matter when, clearly, you don't. You have to let us in or you will be responsible for the fate of your people."

"Madbull, your men are safe—and you know that better than us. How do we know that if and when these men are returned, your troops will not attack us? As far as we are concerned, they are the guarantee of our safety, so we cannot hand them over to you. If you provide a government communication that safe passage will be provided for our people, if that's a possibility, then the handover can happen," asserted the village chief.

"That cannot be arranged," pat came the reply.

"Then our business is done." There was a look of disbelief on the faces of the captives.

"*You* are done, old man. All of you."

"You are committing treason."

"You will hang."

"I think our business is over. Goodnight, officers."

Night came. Colonel Rosie Madbull's men retreated from the gate.

It was a temporary truce. Dusk came and suddenly it was quiet.

An unnatural kind of quiet. Something happening kind of quiet.

Colonel Madbull's men were back in an hour. They gathered outside the village walls.

A new tension prevailed in the air. Some kind of new order had come over. Something decisive was going on. It began soon after.

Bullets are always followed by consequences.

Colonel Madbull decided both.

Three...Two...One...

Fire.

Reload, aim, low.

Lock.

"No, no...! Wait! We are ready to negotiate the release of the hostages in exchange for safe passage for us. In good faith," pleaded Phamdom Lama. He was answered by a blast of gunfire that smashed him against the wall behind him, in parts. The headman lay on the floor, spilling blood and guts.

Three...Two...One...

Fire.

Reload, aim, low.

Lock.

A giant monster seemed to be yanking at the gate. The whole structure shook at the impact. Roared and banged, as they shot indiscriminately. Bricks and mortars chinked everywhere. Incessant firing tore off huge pieces of timber that held the gate up. The bullets moved on after moving through them. Perhaps to make way for the hundreds of metal heads following. They fired so much gunpowder that the soil had charge, was explosive to walk on. The villagers, well, some of them, grew chickenhearted at the sight of the very first charge. From the shots, it seemed the Red-Hounds were in the hundreds; actually, they were about forty, and they came in hordes and went rampaging through the village, firing at all and sundry. The front row, comprising young men, was the first to be hit. The ones who ran to the back, got hit in their backs and the back of the heads, before they could reach the safety of the nearby Iravati river.

Madbull's barbarians had come to rip and maul and slice and gut and rape and slaughter. They yelled and hollered that they would soon string the men by their penises and chop off every child-bearing woman's breast. Such was the rage in their voices, some young children started crying. The women were dead quiet, terrified for their children as the firing continued.

Three...Two...One

Fire.

Reload, aim, low.

Lock.

The wholesale massacre continued for what seemed to be hours, though it was just over twenty-five minutes. No one knew who threw the stones at the regiment. Smashed a soldier's face like a tomato. And then several more stones came flying. Everyone watched in shock. The Red-Hounds chased and caught a group of boys who were responsible, made short work of them with their bullets and bayonets. Till they stopped moving. Till the heat and speed of the bullets broke their skin and shattered their bones and pierced their hearts and their blood came flailing out as red silk flags in a storm.

Headman Lama's son, who had cast not a few stones, in a bid to escape the crazed soldiers, made a mad dash out of the village and managed to reach the nearby nullah, which fed the Iravati river. He jumped into its frothing waters to make good his escape. But he had been spotted and was fired upon. They wounded him. He drifted downstream a few feet and managed to pull himself out by clinging to a rock.

"Don't shoot. Don't shoot. I surrender."

He begged the men when they dragged him, bleeding and part-ripped, to the Colonel. Colonel Madbull smiled and levelled his gun. The headman's son's face blasted off. They came to kill. Not talk. Not reason. The boy was used as target practice for a while by the rest of the men. They got high and wasted on gut sauce and happily pumped him full of lead like he was a pillow. They caught hold of Headman Lama's wife when she was trying to escape from the window of her house. She got trapped on the second floor of her house. They burst in on her, dragged her outside and kept her prisoner till the Colonel came.

"Take her back inside her house," Madbull said. She started screaming and biting like an animal as the men caught hold of her. She was hit on the head with the thick end of a gun and it was a mercy that she was not conscious to see what they did to her.

Madbull's men did more than kill. They tore them up. Broke their fingers to take their rings. The villagers would have willingly parted with each ornament, but the soldiers seemed to enjoy the sound of bones cracking. They cut off their ears to take the gold, scalped them for their hair. Some villagers escaped and hid in the hollows of the trees, buried themselves in the black bog, which soon ran red. They got their first tribesman alive. He was strong and the shine of health could be seen on his face and body. It made them angrier. More determined to crumple it. After kicking and pummelling him to their heart's content, one of the men cut off his ears. He pocketed them as a trophy. The dead man's widow ran out, screaming piercing curses of destruction on the living.

Madbull looked satisfied, and the butchery would have continued, had it not been for the sudden appearance of a visibly distressed Mathera, bearing bad news.

"Out with it, man! What news have you?" asked Madbull.

During the course of the exchange, Madbull's face turned darker and increasingly hostile. The news of Nathan Ray's escape from Baikaal was a deep blow, and seemed to be a special stimulus working upon him. He had the look of a man who had just been told that his work of vengeance had failed spectacularly.

"So, all my enemies are free. Luck shines on my enemies because of the stupidity of the men I employ." His voice pierced through the quiet which had descended.

"I am sorry, Colonel. We were betrayed by our guard."

Madbull's demeanour changed suddenly. "Villagers, you have seen my fury...now, you will see my benevolence. A dangerous man, Nathan Ray, has escaped from Baikaal prison.

He is an anarchist who was plotting against the state. Not just that, the man is responsible for helping the false witch-girl escape! And I have come to know that the guard who helped him get away is a *Habishi*—not from this village, but a *Habishi* all the same. If anyone knows this man's whereabouts, now is the time to speak up and this village will be spared a worse fate. Why, I will even throw in a reward!"

When no one said anything, Madbull warned again.

"They make me look like a fool repeatedly and yet somehow all these affairs are connected to *Habishis*. Someone will have to pay. Where is our informer on Tanu Bakar?"

"It…it was me, Colonel Sir." Sushithal stepped forward as the villagers hissed at his deceit in disgust and horror.

"Come forward. Let me see your face. Aren't you his nephew though? Why would you betray him?"

"For he betrayed me for that witch Amba, Colonel Sir. He humiliated me."

"Aah! An ally against the fake witch! But your information on Tanu Bakar was wrong. You did not betray us for some last-minute emotion, did you?"

"No. I would never do such a thing," Sushithal said.

"Much worth the word of a traitor, when you could betray your own."

He cast a look at Sushithal as one does on a particularly hideous creature. Sushithal stammered, trying to clutch at his self-control. The colour either came to his cheeks or left them, he knew not which.

"Send a team to root him out—him and his men. The weather has turned; he would be hiding in the hills."

"The hills in this weather? Old Patala will get him first!"

"Stop. Such kind of talk is bad for business. Who will want to come here if there are such creatures roaming free? It just scares people—bad for business, very bad." Madbull seethed with malevolent rage. "Mathera...go find that witch and drag her out of her lair by her hair!"

"There are two of them now, Colonel. That militia girl is rumoured to have joined her," Mathera said.

"Then get both of them." Suddenly thoughtful, Madbull wanted to know more about the Witch of Hori.

"This old witch woman—Patala. Why are people so scared of her?"

"They say she is a *phuka*, a shaman. Her mother was one, too," Mathera replied, at which the murmurings among the Red-Hounds increased. The looked about uneasily.

"Does someone still believe in the old wife's tale?" asked one of the soldiers nervously.

"If something has real consequences, it is real."

"But has anyone ever seen her in action?"

"No..."

"I know someone who has heard of her."

"My mother's sister *saw* her."

"Really?"

"White hair, fangs, long nails...She got scared within an inch of her life."

"No. My uncle saw her once. He said she's a skinny woman with big hands and scarred up, knobby feet—"

"He is describing his wife." The attempt at humour fell flat and the mood remained tense.

"I have thought about it at length and have come to the conclusion that she is a shrewd, cunning woman, who has pulled a con trick to fool all. Anyone can do it if they set their mind to it! Or, tell me this, would she not have managed to draw out all the gold from under Hori? Lived like a queen instead of like a wild beast, feeding off berries and roots and

wild animals at the mercy of the elements? She is no witch, nor was that Amba—and they laugh at us, even now as we speak. But we will have the last laugh!"

"What is your information? Tell the Colonel what you told me."

"What is it? The boy has found his tongue again?"

"Sushithal has something to say. He knows where to find the witch."

"You do? You are not fooling us, are you?"

"No, no! I did not say that—how can I know that! He has misunderstood me completely!"

"Boy, doubtlessly you mean to say something, but you have not the resolution to utter it, and only have a cowardly impudence. Speak or die."

"Colonel…Truly, I have nothing to do with the lady in question anymore—"

"Stop your dithering, boy, and don't make me repeat myself. Talk."

Fearful murmurings broke out around him as he walked up to the Colonel.

"Well…I had a lady friend—in the past. She would mention she did some business with the witch. She used to talk about selling her some merchandise for good money. I think she must know where to find her!"

"What exactly is the nature of this merchandise?"

"She could be lying, for all I know! You cannot trust a word they say. She pretended it was only meat but I think she was lying. I mean, why would a witch buy meat from a whore?"

At that, everyone started laughing.

"Maybe it becomes too cold in the mountains."

"I shared this knowledge at great personal risk…" Sushit said.

Mathera opened his mouth to speak and made a sign, a gesture, lifted a finger, as if in warning. But Sushithal ignored him. "I was thinking…it won't be much for a powerful man like you to give me a little reward for my information!"

"A reward, eh?" Madbull asked, his voice plump with hidden menace.

"It's a small thing for you…Colonel…Sir!"

"And what would that be?"

"Just a license to open my own prospector shop, now that our mountain has the yellow metal!" Sushithal said with a sly smile plastered on his face.

"Gold? You want a share in the gold, which is still under the soil?"

"It is, after all, in the land under *our* soil, and the only compensation I beg of you is—"

"Your soil! Your gold! That makes me a robber. Are you calling me a robber, young man? Are you calling Colonel Rosie Madbull a thief?" Madbull smiled widely but it did not reach his eyes and it was frightful.

"No, no…I did not—I am not—God, I dare not—!" Stuttering like a half-wit, Sushithal instantly knew he had just made the biggest mistake of his life. His last mistake. But it was too late. Madbull used his shiny squirrel gun, loaded with a six-inch nail, which plugged straight into Sushithal's neck. Blood burst out of it and he was dead before he hit the ground.

"A warning for the rest of you," Madbull hissed uglily at the villagers. Two red sparks flashed for a moment in his sodden eyes, then flickered out, leaving them dull, glazed and empty. The village women whimpered and drew back in horror.

"We will be back. Be ready with information on my enemies—especially that blackguard Tanu Bakar, and the prison inspector who one of your kind helped escape! If I am pleased,

you will escape the worst. Or, what you just saw will prove to be mild compared to what awaits you and your families."

The brutality of the events which had unfolded for the past few hours had left the villagers stupefied. Women wailed aloud over the injured, the dead; some wailed at the horror of what was to come; some wandered about, frantically bewailing the dead and cursing the living.

When the regiment vehicles began to pull out, Coral appeared from nowhere and blocked their path. One of the constables took out his rifle. Tara scrambled to reign in Coral but, by then, some soldiers had thrown a rope around her neck and begun dragging her into their vehicle. Tara wept and begged for her calf to be spared.

"That's my Coral, sirs. We have nothing left. Please, don't harm her."

Madbull freed the animal and asked Tara, "Is it yours?"

"Yes, sir. She has done no one any harm."

A soldier aimed his gun at the animal.

"You idiot! What are you doing?" shouted Madbull.

"From the looks of it, it seems a crazed animal."

"It is a beautiful creature."

"Sorry, Colonel, my mistake. It is magnificent."

Coral munched grass with a mechanical clapping of the jaw, without removing her gaze from Madbull.

"Hard to imagine, the fire of a pure animal," he said wondrously. "You should appreciate the beast's advantage. Mud-slick and swift, brute strength and hard to catch and kill if they don't want to die. They can thrive on anything; scrap, trash, and still give life-sustaining milk. They look witless and dull, which lulls their enemies. Crafty and clever. But not with me."

Instantly, Madbull aimed his rifle and shot the animal point-blank. Sickening sound of rapid pellets on flesh. Coral let out a wail of agony. She tottered on her feet but, amazingly, did not fall. Nor did she avert her gaze from Madbull. A bullet exploded her head into red and pink. Tara crumpled, stunned; holding her head, she rocked back and forth. After a few more impacts, Coral buckled and lay down.

"I think, if you want to kill something, just do it. Don't write an application, put it on its guard. Just do it. In any case, the beast was too beautiful for these barbarians."

He stood in front of the dying animal. And stared into its eyes. Perhaps he was willing it to remember who sent it to wherever animals went to after death.

In her dying stare, Coral drew back her upper lip in a warning snarl. She too was committing Madbull's hateful face to her memory.

14

Deep inside the Jotsoma, under an endless tangle of gnarled limbs, a strange figure glided forlornly, as if seeking rest from necromantic knots. A menacing alchemy of energy and passions hovered above her like a dense shroud. If one were to put it on paper, it would take the form of such a compelling shape, of a quality that would mesmerise beholders, leave them no choice but to be captive to her being; for she was Patala, the little witch. The slippery precipitous northern heights seemed no match for Patala. She glided with ease through the blinding fog, as if on hooves. Irregularities in the rock pushed into her sole indents and conformed so completely to the shape of the bump, making it impossible for her to slip off the icy surface.

All around her, the rocks and the trees conspired to create a strange vegetation, untouched by commerce or habitation, remote and unvisited. Great tracts of reindeer moss, florets of ancient fauna, lay crisp with frost. Fallen oaks starred with lichen and giant clumps of vicious brambles entwined with screens of hazel and ivy, extending their multitudinous limbs up to the trees to clamber up for light, making the place umbrous with leaves and branches. Impossible for humans to manoeuvre through, but then, she was not one so afflicted. The galloping darkness did not hinder her search for the dhyuti blossom roots, which bloomed in a particular shade of white at this time of the year and had to be dug out under a full moon. Their unique trait of going dormant in bad weather, till things improved, made them difficult to be spotted.

Patala had spent a great part of the day searching, amidst the dense acres that could survive about anything in the world; amidst the milky-white crocus and yellow mottled pigskin, jasmine and cypress roots, but to no avail.

With keen eyes and untiring hands, she checked the forest bed for the elusive herb amongst the stubborn blades of flint forest, washed pewter and bracken stems and pine resin and pitchy vinegar of wood ants. A drizzly wash of dappled pink sprat of phlox looked promising, turned out to be oxblood-leafed sprigs of petunias. The night drew to a close and the only thing of benefit she found were the lime-smelling roots, which flowered once in two years. It would provide the perfect salt to stabilise the colloid she was preparing. She lost track of time and it was only the chirping of the birds, returning to their nests, that warned her of the lateness of the hour.

The dense fog suddenly lifted, as often happens in the mountains, and in the brief moonlight, the distant valley far below shone bright. She stopped to gaze. There was high scorn and curious piety in her gaze. Watching the grim race from the safety of the mountains, she screamed taunts and warnings. Her utterances were underlined by a feeling of betrayal and shame at a city which slept in the bleak bed of its own creation. A crash of lightning threw a lance over the sky and illuminated the dormant city, as if bloated on substances.

The temperature having dropped further, and the scarf wrapped tightly around her face, Patala could barely breathe in the icy wind bloated with crystals. White grains settled on her nose and mouth; their persistence matched only by scorching winds. Making work difficult, the skies opened up briefly and icy water fell in a great swash of release. Convective cloud on a bloated downdraft splashed the ground with water balloons. Seeking shelter, she came to a low-lying stretch of tall reeds, through which she pushed into a dark, thick undergrowth and chuckled with delight. The place was a treasure trove of black berries and succulent roots and she instantly busied herself, turning over rotted logs in search of moist bugs and fungi.

A faint alien odour startled her and she started sniffing about.

When Patala first saw the dead buffalo sprawled behind the rock, she was filled with joy. Succulent bites of flank and sirloin and images of tender loins and crispy brisket floated in her head and her mouth watered, and she realised she was so hungry she could think of nothing else. A buffalo of the size that lay in front her meant food for a whole month for her and her pets. The winter fish she caught at the pond, her chief diet for the last few months, was too bland and bony, and the little flesh which she managed to extricate was chewy as rubber.

Joyous with her find, she hoped the meat would not be too cold to cut. But, to her dismay, she realised that it was beyond her strength to drag the buffalo all the way to her kitchen. Maybe if she cut it into pieces, five or six trips would do it. Holding her knife, she sat on the buffalo, when she suddenly felt something was wrong. Maybe there was a calf inside! That excited her, for tender veal was her favourite meat. Her eagerness was short-lived because the knife refused to sink more than an inch. It seemed to be stuck in some kind of surface—like a cloth, but how was that possible? With a quick movement, she traced the outline of the form.

A human form! How could it be?

It soon dawned on her that whatever was inside the buffalo was definitely not a calf. Her heart raced faster than ever before at the bewitchery, for could there be any other reason to suspect a human body was inside a dead buffalo?

With a smooth flourish of the knife, she cut open the creature's stomach. Out tumbled a young figure with a thick thud. Frozen in solid chunky blood. A girl.

A girl—!

Patala could hardly believe what she saw, for it was common sense, that even if the sun stopped rising in the east, no buffalo would ever swallow a human.

Did the girl climb inside the animal to escape the cold and other predators? For that, she would have had to kill the monster. Judging by the size of the beast, the girl must have been exceptionally strong to be able to do that.

Little good it seemed to have done the girl, the way she ended up all covered in solidified blood, inert, dead. What a waste, Patala thought. All craving for buffalo meat left her and she turned to go. The forest would make short work of both. She turned to go and then she felt it.

A breath.

A whisper.

It could have been the movement of air.

Something made her stop. With great difficulty, she managed to make the girl lie on her back. The girl's eyes were open and without focus. She was staring at an imaginary point in space. An empty cicada shell. Lifeless. Almost. And when the girl blinked, Patala thought it was the most wondrous thing she had seen in a long time.

What Patala was not prepared for was the strange and sudden pulsation which ran in a current through her body. She felt several voices speak to her and they sounded louder than a sudden shotgun blast in the rainstorm.

⌘ PROPHECIES ⌘

Meeting with Maha Shamanka was Her fate. A prophecy. Even though We were inside Her, We felt Maha Shamanka's mystic power. We were mesmerised. There were many more prophecies for later. But it was fated that Maha Shamanka would nudge Her through the ordeal of Her adolescence—from what She thought as freedom to what growing up would mean, with the necromantic knots growing inside Her.

The re-shaping commenced in Her unconscious state. She came back with isolated pockets of memory. Each containing a different version of Her. There were versions of Her to whom bad things had happened and then there were also versions of Her to whom the bad things did not happen. She looked at Her life and saw clones of Herself, each having bits of Her and the sum of Them was more than Her. This terrified Her, because if there were so many of Her, which one was She? Were They false and Her current self real or was Her current self false and it was one of the others standing in the line who was real?

We tried to chat with Her. She seemed confused. The voice was a soft parting of the air, the most beautiful thing We had ever heard.

"Who are you?" She asked Us finally.

"We are all kinds. In between, too god too human, too half-way spirit bastards."

"Why me?" She asked.

"Deity seed, You know Your truth."

"Since when have you been inside me?" She asked.

"We began with You," We replied.

"How is it possible?" She had doubts.

"It was easy. You are so turgid with potential and yet so empty with spaces under Your skin and inside Your marrows—So much room for Us to yawn into existence," We replied.

"Even though you were curled and inactive inside, I could already feel the unsettling your presence caused; the nightmares and terrifying dreams, all of it was you?" She asked with wonder.

"Not all, but most, yes," We replied.

"What do you even want from me?" She asked.

"Accept Us—use your gift," We replied.

"What else?"

"Blood, belief and sacrifice will be required," We replied.

"Are you warning me?"

"Is a nudge a warning?"

"The gift, which I have not asked for, nor begun to understand nor use, what if I don't use it?" She asked

"There was a shelf life to being a god-spawn, and if You waste Your gift, it's not that some unseen golden scales would be shed. But, then, you would be reduced to a useless husk, living a meaningless futile life. For, of what use is a light, harmless, helpless husk?" We replied.

Her slate was suspended in the light even as fine grains of Her spirit particles moved randomly as thought phantoms. Dismembered one instant, whole the next. At once still, changing as well.

Her mind was a mushy bowl of loose gruel, lacking framework. Her slate was transformed into a raging sea of sensations, crashing into the shores of Her mental tissue, tearing, searing, piercing Her nerves. The immediate exterior of Her slate was sliced away. They flowed past Her memories. She went back and forth and then right to the day when, after being gobbled by clouds for weeks, the sun came out with such force that the town turned an eerie white on that fateful day.

15

Probably the dreams had started even while she was walking. Amba saw herself floating inside the carbonised skeleton of her childhood home. The blurry vision of the dream gave everything a furry tint, like algae on the cliff face. She put out a hand to touch the charred wood. The air became flat, and the nature of space around the people in it was two-dimensional to emphasise a raging nightmare. Eighteen years ago, on this day, Mother and Father had burned themselves to death. Her secret memory box opened and thoughts spilled out like impatient children during lunch break.

It started as an ordinary day. Contourless from the cold in her lungs and a persistent cough, Mother's face was strangely drawn when she told her to run an errand. She had been like that since the night she was gangraped. Avoiding Mother's sorrow-laced eyes, she watched herself take the five coins to get some rice from the market. On her return, the main door was ajar and extremely hot to the touch. The fire was still raging inside. The stone floor was cracked into pieces from the blaze, windows black with soot, furniture twisted out of shape, photographs charred. Walls had peeled off in portions to reveal blistered layers. Their bodies lay burning on the bed. Nakul sat curled up in one corner, immune to the fact that the fire was devouring his clothes. Amba had to pry his fingers loose from the burning quilt wrapped around their mother, but from then on, Nakul was possessed with a desolation which would grip him with increasing force over time. She watched everything from afar and yet her emotions formed the core mass of her dream. Amba managed to save him from certain death that day, but as it would turn out, she could not save him from life.

On the fifth day of her stupor, the pain blowback reached a breaking point and Amba's fever broke with a spray of beaded perspiration on her brow and nose. Her body felt limp and supple with the drug and she could only groan. A peculiar red darkness on her eyes meant that the sun was shining bright through her closed lids. She opened her eyes and the dazzling sunlight made her moan in pain, forcing her to snap them back shut; slowly, she eased them open, giving them time to adjust. Eventually, the depths began to contract and the light began to grow brighter and the surrounding objects came into view and the walls of the room she was in, swayed. The whiff of menace in the air was very real.

Instantly, Amba became conscious of another presence in the room. The shock of it made her look away and then back again, drawn by a force, towards the strange woman. Her eyes were very thin, almost elongated. Their eyes met and a gush of incredulous familiarity engulfed Amba. She went through an emotion beyond comprehension and remained suspended in disbelief. Without being told, she knew she was in the presence of Patala, the little witch. Mercifully, no forked tongue flicked from her lips, nor were there writhing snakes as thin as worms on her head.

"You were sleeping so peacefully I almost did not want to wake you up. Was it wonderful what you were dreaming of?

Or dreadful? I have dreams, too, and I could let myself dissolve in them, let them take me over…but dreams and nightmares aren't all there is. We have to wake up at some point." Patala's voice thrummed with the charge of a hundred fully grown buffaloes.

"Girl, you look disappointed! What did you expect—wings snaking around my back and scales on my legs and ten-inch talons?" Patala joked and Amba was too stunned to reply.

The old witch's petite body was an abstract sculpture of bones, thinly wrapped in parchment skin, so often torn and tapered that one could see the seams sewn along her flesh. Her skin was surprisingly smooth and pale, as of one who stays underground most of the time, and her cheekbones stood out as a skull-bone. She had heavy, wet, black hair and she was dressed in a plain cotton smock, more suitable for nightwear. There was a stillness around her mouth which seemed sealed shut, her eyes seemed not to have known sleep for an eternity. Under the bulge of her forehead, her eyes were lost and the rest of her face was hidden under the lank hair around her ears, down to the prominent cut of her jaw. A small gold tuft of hair hung under her chin. If one looked closely, it was a hair-covered appendage of flesh around her throat. In the day time, her eyes were oddly horizontal, with rectangular pupils and the side-slanted eyes for a wider field of vision—not much different from hers.

There was a distinct pre-historic scent to Patala and it caught in Amba's nose—peppery, rusty as a storm rain. Amba found her beautiful in a strange way, her eyes fiery, almost orange-brown, formidable like a granite cliff, a thunder cloud. Her presence filled the room. Wild and reptilian was her gaze when she turned her head to stare at Amba, unblinking.

Guarding its mistress, a dark shaggy wolf-like creature stood half-bare in the snow—but it was not alone. They were soon surrounded by a whole pack of such creatures. Wind-rough and shiny from the sun. Impossibly muscular limbs thickly calloused, their bodies puckered with old and new scars, and no more than seven feet in height. Covered with scars from many previous fights. Were these the creatures the shamans spoke of in whispers—the *Tengoo*, she wondered—the mythical ambush predators—half-wolf half-dog guardian demons of the Hori mountain! Due to the combination of the olive-green fur and the brown stripes across their backs, they were virtually invisible among the bush and tall grasses their prey fed upon.

"Don't be scared. They will not harm you. Domovai is their queen. They do her bidding. She is very gentle for a *Tengoo*!" She assured Amba that the *Tengoo* were not the enemy of the people of the hills and that there were no better protectors of the mountains and forests, harbingers of windfalls to benefactors and calamities to humans intruding upon their domains. In the village, they would say that no one had ever seen a *Tengoo* and lived to tell the tale; all some hunters managed to glimpse was a massive tail disappearing into the dark, or fangs at six feet, or the memory of an eye, the colour of hell, waiting to devour their living flesh. The phantom beasts gained infamy over time, fattened on the words of scared men on their deathbeds. The myth grew bigger, the beast more monstrous and the woman who could control such demonic beasts more terrifying.

It was all too much to take for Amba and she sat down.

"Who are you?" Amba croaked out the needless question.

"But you know who I am, don't you?" Patala gazed at her and chuckled sarcastically. Amba tried not to look shocked.

"Your people have been fed rubbish about witches. About us having pointed teeth, blood-stained mouths which makes one shudder, the whole carnal and unspirited appearance. You should know better. A witch always recognises her kind. I am the one they call the Witch of the Jotsoma, the one they are scared to name!"

"I am no witch," Amba shot back, anger replacing fear.

It felt good. To be angry. Anger gave her some semblance of control.

"Not just a witch. My girl, you are a warrior witch. A very unusual witch—one of a kind!" Patala retorted, adding, "Domovai senses your witch. That's why she did not attack you."

Amba was speechless.

"You will learn to accept your witch," Patala said. "The sooner the better for you. If you don't, you are weak and blind because you choose to die. You will be sorry in the end," Patala said, fingering the amulet around her neck. Amba had heard tales about the strange-looking ornament from the village shamans—they called it 'the living eye of a *Tengoo*'. It was said to have magical powers to ward off calamities for whoever wore it, if the wearer was deemed worthy of it. Voices swept through Amba's mind. She rolled in the words, dived into them, emerged, and was one with them. She simply could not help it and was furious at her helplessness in front of Patala.

"You have the sign of the powers of heaven and earth. You are blessed differently. Have you not heard the voices?"

"No. There are no voices. I don't know what you are talking about."

"Are you going to just stand there and lie that you don't hear those voices inside you?"

Amba *had* lied. In the streets of Hori, having a world inside of her was a thing to hide. To hate. She knew about hate. About fear. Why should it be any different here? But when Patala called her a witch, it did not sound like a slur. The word was not wrapped in an arrogant smirk. The word was uttered as a simple recording of a fact.

Amba did not know how to react. That someone could wield such knowledge about her so casually, she had never imagined. Nor did she try to fathom the nature of the sympathy which existed between her and the little witch. Patala held her hand and led her slowly to the garden and Amba found herself following, like a child with no will of her own. Amba looked about her. The garden was soaked in a mysterious calmness. Giant crocus and poppy and hogweed, mandrake and even some cannabis and henbane—a chronicle of the sinister side of the plant world.

"Don't be afraid. I am just stocking up to rid of the pains."

"The smell— *blaargh*!" Amba retched.

"That's the sumac!" Patala pointed at the thick, small viridian bushes with pointed leaves. "It produces white fruits, smells shitty, and the viler the swamp, the better it grows and, to my utter joy, I find it eats away pain. It would have withered and died, had I not restored it to life."

Patala's sense of nomenclature was evident in the special treatment she had given to the herbs and the over-tended exotic ferns over the lowly ferns, daisies and mimosas.

"Pretentious little beasts," she said of the pretty but useless juleps, smelling of sweet alcohol and trailing blue periwinkles, setting them against the shocking orange of the nasturtiums and scarlet potted poinsettias and many more, which Amba was seeing for the first time in her life. A strange-looking plant held her attention. Hidden in its bulbous stems were unusual flowers, of different smells. One sweet and the other mouldy.

"Oh, you have found her? So ordinary, yet so wicked. The dose makes the poison or the healant. As skin does, the way it lends itself to a body—it becomes a permanent barrier to healing, constantly gouging out goodness from your flesh, until too late!"

A fish pond was installed in the leafy part of the garden. The inhabitants, round blobs of prickly flesh, looked bloated from every end. Probably from eating more than they would ever get to eat in their natural habitat, she thought.

"She and her children have contributed a lot to science, if you know what I mean. I have other scientific-minded friends too. If only I had a human to test my medicines on, the results would come out so much better! A pig behaves as a pig will. I used to have monkeys at one time. To get a human would be excellent. I need to see what works and what doesn't—"

Amba stepped back in alarm.

"Don't be scared! I don't mean any harm to a fellow witch." Patala smiled.

Stop calling me that, Amba wanted to scream.

I am NOT a witch!

Outside, the murk came back and transformed the dusk into a thing of demonic beauty. The red sun, sliding down the distant barren hill, and the haze turned the western sky into a nosebleed. By the time the lights on the mountain got brighter, Patala prepared a special feast—maguey fruit and crispy red fish—and drank the maguey juice, which would have intoxicated a lesser mind.

Patala drew out a handful of suet, of some unrecognisable meat, which she sucked in meditative silence. By now, deep hunger was gnawing inside Amba's stomach so she ate the meat without questioning. Imperceptibly, her eyes settled into a watching Domovai, who hungrily devoured a good-sized piece of meat. Patala tossed her another piece, bony and dripping with blood, and Domovai scrambled with it into a corner.

The animal unnerved Amba. To her, Domovai and her pack seemed a thing of death; spooky, pale-eyed psychopaths. Amba could swear she looked larger in size than she did at dawn, when she first saw her. Had Domovai gained height as the sun went down? What other freakish peculiarities did Patala's pet possess? And worse, what other horrors breathed in Patala's abode? Amba had no intention of finding out. Her instinct to make distance from the little witch and her monstrosities was overriding. There was little choice but to bide her time for now.

That night, she dreamt of heads of several black crows bubbling in burning lead and a grey, dusty Patala pouring her concoctions down her throat, till her bowels burst and blood leaked out of her ears, even as Domovai fixed her with the stony stare of a sphinx across aching and eternal desert sands.

16

Devil Spit was a sordid little dope spot, seeped in menace, where every second man seemed a second away from a drink in the face or a bullet in the back. A seedy establishment inhabited by prostitutes, hustlers and pimps, plying their trade among a gathering of out-of-work criminals, drunks and addicts, haggling with the bartender, who put drinks on tabs that shouldn't exist in this crummy part of the world. The proceedings were aptly summed up in the graffiti sprayed on a wall, in neon, blinking, 'Sex! Sex! Sex!'

The place took on an entirely different sort of grit when the sun set. Exactly the place to find Manimal, Mathera thought with a grimace. He disliked Manimal with his warthog-pig looks. Wiry and pockmarked, and nostrils that snorted coke like they were vacuum cleaners.

"Damn shithole! She had better not be a waste of time," Mathera cursed.

"This is a fine establishment run by a fine woman with a remarkable sense of business."

"Business? For grave robbers and fuck-wads who owe money to everyone kind of business?"

"Not everyone can afford to be choosy. Besides, everyone needs a bar. As a bonus, you get to hear the familiar slurs of your mother tongue."

Over this part of the valley, the sky was peculiar; a hideous yellow cast with specks where the clouds had defecated. Under its asbestos pillars, a group of thin and plump, bare-headed and draggled, highly made-up girls with the debauched eyes of women were conducting their business with mannerisms of those bound by an iron-clad fate. A yellow-complexioned girl sorted them out as potential clients.

"Want to have sex?"

"Get lost, whore. You don't have what I want."

"C'mon, what is your delight?" Twins with long, straight, black hair stuck out their tongues and shouted "Woohoo" and stroked each other's backs. In reality, not very different from the drunk and doped people streaming about, their faces marked and gait heavy with opiates.

Mathera drew a pistol and checked to see if the magazine was full before he slid it back in its holster.

"We are looking for Candy," said Manimal.

"You found her," a waiter pointed at a woman on the stage.

The bright-pink tones of the 'stage' ludicrously stood out against the grunginess and dark squalor of the overcrowded tavern. The room was midnight blue, filled with inventive sexual imagery. The woman on the stage started to undress a man. She unbuttoned his shirt and cuffed him to a wall. She pulled her dress up over her breasts and straddled him. They mimed sex. Entwined in phony ecstasy, they gasped and screamed in fake pleasure. It was a depressing act to witness and looked more comical than sexual.

"I hear you got some business with Candy?"

Mathera turned around to be confronted by a metal-toothed man, with his name, presumably Stud, tattooed on his chest, barring their way. His shoulder-length hair was tied in a ponytail, which hung limp and greasy under his fancy cap.

"And who might you be?"

"Stud," he said, pointing to his tattoo with a smirk. "You have to go through me if you want to conduct business with Ms Candy."

"Really? You the boss?" asked Mathera. His words were uttered simply and seemed to carry no malice, though, perhaps, that is what malice sounded like in those perfect tones. But steeped in substances, Stud failed to sense the danger he was in.

"Yeah, that too. Boss for you. I am her manager, too. I handle this business establishment—aahh! Get away from me, you runt-faced faggot trash—stop please!"

Stud screamed in anger and agony. Mathera had Stud's crotch in a pincer grip and gave it a vicious tug. It achieved the desired result and affected a profound change in Stud's deportment and, between sobs of pain, he apologised profusely for his lack of manners.

Candy was produced in front of the two men and the area vacated without much ado. Her eyes were open and shone with substance-induced fever but, despite the lavender circles under her eyes and her bleach-blonde hair slam-dunked to one side of her head, she held a curious attraction.

"You want to talk to me, handsome?"

Candy's voice tinkled with fake laughter as she pointed at her name, spelled out in shiny gold alphabets on a thick chain around her neck.

On proximity, her age became an assumption; she was in that indeterminate period of middle age that calls attention to its own indeterminacy. Mathera was expecting a whore with a filthy dress and purple shadows under her eyes, stinking of opium; he was relieved that she was the opposite, in fact, she seemed to be in good health and spirits.

Candy had a vixen quality to her features, her eyes slanted slightly and her nose curved upwards in a way that called to mind some alert and inquisitive creature, not entirely without intelligence. Her lips were full, her teeth delicately shaped, spaced evenly, and her hair was bright copper, that colour called red by men, that darkened with movement. Her rouged cheeks and titillated aspect was manufactured in the moments prior to their entrance.

"So, talk," she spoke as one for whom the appearance of friendliness was worth it only to initiate some sort of reciprocal cooperation.

"You have been keeping interesting company."

"Meaning what?"

"That should be meaning 'who'."

"What is in it for *me*, handsome? Why should I tell you about what company I keep?"

Their initial idea that she was a beauty queen took a hit. He guessed her to be in her late thirties, added five years when he saw the dark age spots on the thinning skin under her eyes.

"Nothing. Except perhaps you save yourself a well-deserved hiding, whore."

A look flashed in his eyes like teeth in a wolf's mouth.

"Who the fuck are you?" she mumbled, scratching her pock-marked face, with no particular interest in an answer, and went back to watching a video on her phone. If the staginess of the acting made Mathera cringe, the accidental humour forced a smile out of him. The act possessed a bizarre appeal, as a deformed child who insists on running the race.

"Am I in trouble?" she asked, when they identified themselves. "I have lots of younger ones too. Untouched."

Her pitch dropped two levels to almost casually intimate. Her eyes glittered with a slyness one sees in delinquents pretending to be harmless pups.

"I will not touch what you have to offer with a bargepole, whore. Let us not waste time. We hear you've been doing business with witches."

Candy opened her mouth and then closed it, and her eyes bulged.

"I been doing no such thing. I am not friends with no witch." She said in a hurry.

"You've been helping enemy of the state."

"Enemy of the state—I never helped any enemy. Who am I to help anyone?" Candy said in a thin voice.

"Are you sure? Because we have information which completely implicates you."

"Unless you are talking about the business I was in from many years."

"And?"

"She would buy goats and pigs from me."

"For what?"

"To eat, I assumed."

"Assumed?"

"In the beginning, it was fine. Then she wanted monkeys. No one eats monkeys. So I was a bit suspicious what she needed the monkeys for."

"You got her monkeys?"

"She paid good money. She paid maximum for the monkeys."

Mathera put down his glass of brandy and cracked his knuckles in an intimidating way.

"What do you mean by she took monkeys? Which monkeys?" he tried not to sound incredulous.

"All kinds. She said they were the closest to human beings, so...She said she wanted to test her medicines and such."

"Test her medicines on poor captive animals? And you helped her! That's guilty, from where I see."

"A very big crime," Manimal added.

"No...Sir, wait! Let me explain. That's my boy there. He was bedridden. Polio in both feet and hands. Her medicines cured him. He can now walk and run with men half his age!"

"Black magic, it seems. You fraternised with a witch, madam. You sold her monkeys for her torturous goings-on. You are in serious trouble."

There was a scary quality in the way he spoke. Candy looked increasingly unsettled.

"I have nothing to do with the witch." Her cheery and effusive tone became distrustful and scared. "I am a businesswoman. She wanted the meat and the animals and I had the best stock. I haven't done any business with her for a long time now. It was so long ago—years ago—I did not even know who she was, just that she was good with medicines, that's all. I swear...!"

"Stupid whore, one becomes bound to what one says in front of a police officer. Bound to the repercussions of what you say—truth or lie—and if you lie, you have to keep on lying and compound it with smaller lies, getting caught in the chain reaction of your own lazy mistake."

"No, no, no, I don't know anything! I never met her again. She warned me never to set foot on her mountain, so I am scared," she said sobbing. She made noises of alarm when pressed with questions and answered with deep exhaustion that showed as a tremor in her throat.

"Stop playing us for fools, you ugly whore. Selling poisoned tar to witches. Better still, let's take this whore to jail! Maybe she will like the company. The men there have not seen a whore for such a long time."

"Years. Many, many years," said Manimal.

"No! Sirs, I beg of you. I am no criminal! I am just a hard-working businesswoman! Ask anyone."

"So, run your business at Baikaal, woman! You will definitely cheer up lots of inmates."

Candy shrank back. Her hands moved to her mouth in shock and horror and she wailed piteously.

"Anything, not t-that, sirs, please! A-anything, not that! I will help you. I will tell you where she lives, please, sirs. I will point out her damned pit to you— Just not there! I done no crime. I am no thief. I am no criminal, sirs!"

"One more thing…Why did you stop doing business with her if it was so profitable?"

"I did not. She did. Said I was drugging the animals to make them look healthy and warned me to not to do it again or she would curse me. I am not as strong and brave as you, sirs, with your weapons and all, to deal with a witch. I'm just a poor hard-working businesswoman—"

None of the men noticed the sly look in Candy's eyes. It was the contented smile of a shrewd woman who had successfully dispatched her inquisitors to their damnation.

17

The rancid smell of wild boldo suffused the cellar air. Acidic salt and virgin alder sticks, soaked overnight in burning mustard oil, bubbled over a slow fire with the sole purpose of banishing evil spirits. The arid outside never penetrated the stone walls of Patala's basement lab, nor the dust, nor the sun.

Amba stopped among the rambling stone passages near the entry to the substructure, uncertain which way to turn next. Patala's strange chants reached her ears. Intrigued, she climbed upon the roof and peered down the black depths of the chimney. The scene did not make much sense to her at first, for surrounded by flat tables and three clocks, exactly timed, on each side, Patala was measuring out powders and intermittently grinding portions on the stone mortar with a heavy pestle. Amba's gaze followed the little witch as she meticulously poured coloured char-boiled mixtures into tiny calibrated containers, which smoked and crackled. On her busy desk, the increasing number of small pots, spilling over with mixtures, looked like an advancing army.

Patala was invoking *Bhadloki*, the fearsome androgynous deity of the netherworld, probably to preside over some demonic act she was about to commit. Devouring noxious octli juices, straight from bloated maguey kernels, which she held with her long-fingered hands, the little witch was swaying to the muggy thumps of unseen drums. Azure sinter fell off in formless clumps as she danced and sang in the flickering light, looking no less ferocious than her demonic pets. Staring limply in a corner was the monstrous Domovai, whose spirit gave the effect of having turned to ash as amorphous as the blue mountain soot smeared on the old witch's skin. The words uttered by Patala filled her with growing unease.

Lurk...under the veil...of black...mist...lingers...it conceals my dark desire...while I wait...I will be sated...for in my sight...looms... she full of despair...in my dwelling...she cowers...taking solace...in slumber...the very chamber that shelters her...will soon...become... her...grave...her wails of pain will feed my soul...her nightmares will make me grow strong...as she...grows weak...I gnaw...I feast...

I feast on her sinew...and bones...she can see her own end...and so...can...I and at last...my hunger lessens...my desire...grows...I crave...for more...and I wait again for a reckless soul...to find me... yet...another...

The true import of the words slowly sunk in. Amba had heard enough.

Panic gripped her and, grabbing a torch, a bottle of water and her gun, she crept out of the back door—the front being bolted shut. Stumbling into tarred darkness, her torch threw a dim white light over a new territory—a cavernous, icy-cold passageway, low ceilinged and dusty and bare. The torch light slapped crazy patterns across the walls, of strange creatures with breath which hung as sea fog in the air. Dead rats lay inverted, brittle and bloated with ice, their edges dimmed with condensation.

Within no time, she stood at the edge of the forest; before her lay the unknown deeps of the Jotsoma, behind her were Patala and her perverse creatures. Straining to hear past the beat of her own heart and the thrum of her own blood, Amba pressed on. She tried not to think of the predators on the prowl and monstrous leviathans crawling up and down the hillside, and multi-pod hollow sac night-worms, squirming out of their holes, pressing their cold, wet multi-faces on everything. Unseen creatures seemed ready to spring upon her from the dark and huge-rooted trees blocked her footing; knotted climbers, of the girth of a man's limbs, hung from branch to branch in tangled masses like snakes.

Stumbling forward, in a near-hydrocephalic haze, into the darkness, it was not long before she started cursing herself for her stupidity. Her skin crawled with fear every time brittle leaves snapped under her feet and brambles left little red slashes on her neck and deposited slithering reptiles in her hair. Her legs tensed to flee and she already longed to scramble back to the safety of the known world. But it was too late now to turn back. Exacerbating her precarious situation was the sudden rainstorm, which stung like bees and completely blinded her. It gathered on all sides, brown with the sludge and driftwood, and the innumerable cuts on the exposed parts of her skin from the sharp brambles were on fire.

The bog was well hidden, and by the time she realised the danger, it was too late. Amba was hopelessly trapped. Sinking. She kicked hard to surface above the thick black waters. But the current was a barbed wire with its hooks in her. And, with its hundred claws, it sliced and chopped at her flesh, lacerating her exposed skin. A fox, sucked into the waters, ripped by the swirling debris, went bleating and whipping and thrashing into the distance, a brief flash bobbing back and forth and then it was gone. She could not let go. Until the wind quietened down to erratic coughs, until the sky brightened from sick orange to clean slate, until the milling water around her receded, she refused to let go of her safe spot. The wood felt spongy and she knew she must move before the current picked up again. She slid sidewards into the maw of a maze, leaving behind her a thin wake. Amba looked up over the lip of the brush and could see that bushes were cleared away from the ground to knee level. Her shoes were gone, sucked out when the water tried to rip off her skin, which she did not give as it was attached to her bones.

Then, her worst nightmare came true. The ground gave away altogether. In an instant, she was deep inside the black, shitty water and each panicky thrust of her legs spun the brambles, and the strong undercurrent of water dragged her face first into the bog. It swirled her round and round into the centre, towards the gullet of the bog, from where there could be no escape.

Body stretched taut like a hawser ready to crack, Amba spinned, kicked, jerked and grabbed at water to keep her head above. The whirlpool was all teeth. It would not let go. There was not a thing her exhausted body could do and a muffled sob escaped from her throat, and that's when she felt a powerful tug.

It was Domovai, leaning and leaning, further and further towards her. The beast stretched her massive neck as far as it would go and opened her jaws, but could not reach Amba. Domovai overbalanced and scrambled upright. A change in tactics was required. She then made a cobra-strike grab for Amba with one great, grasping foot. Her reach was astonishing, her legs almost as long as she was. A muscled shin, tawny as a lion's, lashed out, and her talons caught Amba's dress. It was a killer clasp. Teeth, which, with one snap, could tear her from limb to limb. Domovai felt the pulsating, demonic strength of them and surrendered. But there was something about the force of it that made Amba thankful she was alive.

"Even witches die, you know," Patala scolded her. "You should thank Domovai for your life."

The beast growled when she heard her name. Back at the tavern, safe and warm and dry, Amba felt foolish. She had survived a great ordeal but it was of her own making. She touched the talon incision, a half-inch long, deep slash, right on her thighs where Domovai had gripped her. She pressed the place hard with her fingers till it stopped bleeding.

"You gave us a fright. Where did you think you would reach if you went out into the Jotsoma at this time of the night? Even *I* won't be that foolish."

Patala shook her head and emptied a sweet tincture down Amba's throat. Waves of pain ran cold and hot, then cold again, and she shook with fever and the hours passed. Her limbs were raw and blackened, her back bubbled with sores. She fell into a stupor and dreamt of the woods that would hide her, the mossy ground soft against her ravaged skin. The air in the woods was salty and stabbed like needles, and each touch of the wind set her burns screaming again. She closed her eyes, drifting through the shocks and skirls of pain.

It might have been some trick of the fire; the light flickered on Patala's face as she drew closer. She took out a small jar of sealed wax and touched her finger to the liquid inside, then pressed the finger to Amba's face and said something, too low to be heard. Amba's skin itched and hummed. When she put her finger to her cheek, though, it felt smooth.

"What is it that you said when you touched my skin?"

"A word of knowledge."

"Will you teach me?"

"The gift cannot be taught. Either you find it yourself or you do not."

Amba gazed at her hands. Slowly, her breath eased and her eyes cleared. Her arms and legs still ached when she brushed them with her fingers. She touched skin instead of leather.

"A little more and it would be poison. You see, the correct dose is the first key," Patala remarked.

Amba tried not to choke on the air suffused with sulphurs and phosphorus and quicklime, as she emptied the sweetly potent liquor of unidentifiable components into her mouth, and reeled back in shock from the stab she felt in her stomach. The jolt was intense. It sobered her.

"Feel this."

Amba drew back nervously.

"Don't be scared. You must try. I did too!"

"I am not anything like you. I am not a witch," Amba said dully.

"I am not a witch either!" Patala said and broke out into high-pitched laughter, which startled the birds.

"You are like that scared little bird who closes its eyes and thinks the danger is gone. How ridiculous that you are supposed to be a warrior!" Patala taunted again.

"Accept your witch, girl, before it's too late."

Accept your witch.

Amba felt hot and angry.

"Even if the world contained powers, why would it, of all the people, fall on someone such as me to discover it?"

"Why *not* you? Tell me—why not you? You have to accept the *gift* or it will rot, or worse, get out of control and become a deadly curse. You doubt too much, that is your curse."

The gift cannot be taught. Either you find it yourself or you do not.

Amba thought of the humming inside her head when she touched objects, the eerie knowledge that had guided her all her life.

She looked at her hands.

"If you have it, you practice. Or you don't. And lose it. There is no tearing hurry. Accepting your *gift* is simply adding a new sense—the body needs time to adjust," Patala said.

Amba sighed and sat back at the long table, watching Patala put together a manual of potions and, at times, get angry at herself at mixing up empirical readings. She plucked the purple buds and tore them from their stems and smashed them between her palms; the tiny thorns pierced her skin and the sap bled in and mixed with her blood, but she didn't care. Patala opened her stained palms and stared at the broken skin. She shut her palms. She wasn't really seeing anything. Her hands opened and shut and opened and shut. The next time they opened, the blood was gone.

"I can't do all this. I know nothing," Amba said.

"Witchery is not about summoning dragons and serpents! Or converting an oak seedling into a red strawberry…or bringing a withered flower back to life…or blossoming cherries out of season or turning the fire vivid green. But your witches are your matter. Your business with them is yours." Patala said and, without any warning, blew yellow pollen from a flowery herb into Amba's face. A pollen so potent that flowers sprung wherever it fell.

Amba's ears were suddenly humming and her head was a hive. A pain gnawed at her chest and she pressed her hands to it, the hollow and the hard bones. And Patala pressed the strange-looking herb into her hand.

A different feeling now surged within her. A new syncing.

For a start, she felt multiple colour sensitivities in her eye; she could watch thermals of warm air rise, roil and spill into clouds, and trace too, the magnetic lines of force that stretched across the earth.

The light falling into her deep, dark pupils was registered with such frightening precision that she could see, with fierce clarity, things she would not have possibly resolved from the generalised blur. Her fragile human eyes were overwhelmed by the light, the details, while the *witch* inside watched everything with the greedy intensity of a child filling the colouring book.

But, in a few moments, Amba could feel all the insight leaving her. She felt nauseous. And clammy. Enveloped with a feeling of a huge loss. Her tongue felt thick and furry and tarred. The knowledge was gone.

She was empty.

She was emptied out.

"You have to work at it to receive it. As any *gift*, it will wilt and vanish if you don't receive and honour it," Patala said. "Gods and beasts would be revealed to you, Mother would say, and it would be up to you to choose who you talk to. I learned a lot more than Mother wanted. About the world of spirits—some good, some really bad."

Patala's mother, and her mother before that, were noted shamans, chief healers of the inhabitants of Hori. Women of infinite intelligence. The sick discarded as untreatable, those with terrible wounds, ugliest of sores, set bones, fevered minds, all came to them. Though painfully slow, their remedies were sure.

"I started from ignorance. Knew nothing except fire, which produces light. She spared no pains to set forth all that pertains to its nature—the manner of its production and support, and to explain how heat was sometimes found without light, and light without heat; to show how it can induce various colours upon different bodies and other diverse qualities; how it reduces some to a liquid state and hardens others; how it can consume almost all bodies, or convert them into ashes and smoke; and finally, how, from these ashes, by the mere intensity of its action, it forms glass, for, as this transmutation of ashes into glass appeared to me as wonderful as any other in nature, she took a special pleasure in describing it."

Patala looked wistful as she thought of her mother, and for some time, it looked like that was all she would speak. But then, she spoke in a freshly determined way.

"My mother would speak of the earth in particular. It was wondrous to hear from her how, with water and air on its surface, the disposition of the heavens and heavenly bodies, more especially of the moon, must cause a flow and ebb like in the seas, and the unviolated flow of winds between tropics. She taught me how the mountains, seas and rivers were naturally formed on earth; and the metals produced in the mines, and the plants grown in the fields, and in general, how all the bodies, which are commonly denominated mixed or composite, organic and inorganic, might be generated from the stars in the heavens! That what we have within us is from the stars of the cosmos, and how every being is connected to the other by a unique light and how the same rules govern our bodies. She knew so much; she was kind and she taught me and would have taught me so much more..."

"What happened to her?" asked Amba, eager to know more.

"They wanted her to sell her farm to the Regiment. She refused. In a week, they spread rumours about her, called her a phuka. And there was no place for a witch who worshipped Loki, the underworld god. Because the phuka were child-eaters and snatchers of youth. They hung her. This is the only thing I have to remember her by..." she said, stroking her only adornment, a blue-green crystal clouded with beads, hanging from her neck.

Patala said sorrowfully, as if recalling the day she found her mother hanging from the village tree, "She paid the price for knowing too much." And added, with a faraway look in her eyes, "As I will, too."

"Buffalo soup tonight," Patala said, pointing at the dead buffalo.

Ghostly pins of light, sliced by the blind, fell on places where the earth had split open due to the heat. Assigning Amba her new duty, Patala busied herself, measuring out ingredients for her potions. Domovai yawned and put her head on her giant paws, her snores drowning out forest sounds.

"You will have to make a pyre first. Get on with it, then, girl!" muttered Patala. Realising she was on her own, Amba got down to work. She made a sledge out of a thick canvas cloth, dragged the carcass down the broken road path, the stones worn smooth with the passage of time and ravage of the elements. Cedar and yew and mountain ash, that she chopped herself, their white pith spraying where the axe blade struck. She built a pyre under Patala's watchful gaze. Piled it high with wood till she was satisfied. Next, she lifted the buffalo's body, which seemed to be growing heavier by the second. She pulled it up to the pyre's top and lit the flames. The reddish-brown insides of the beast stood exposed; its edges encrusted with grunge. Clusters of small insects whirred and hovered over something juicy and dead.

"Hurry up, girl. I am hungry too. I have not eaten for long."

But there was no wind and the air was wet and the flames fed slowly. It took the whole afternoon for the carcass to even blacken. And a day more for it to burn down to ash. She watched until the last flame was gone. Gradually, it blended with the tarty odour of the boab maguey fruit, readied to be mixed in the plump, red meat fried earlier in the morning. A whirring sound made her start and she looked over her shoulder with a shudder. It was just a big, fat beetle, with a gorged, inflated stomach, getting ready to settle down on a fat-coated wall, which had turned white with heat. Despite the huge bonfire, shadows were gathering around the corners.

"Eat. Spirits need to be fed for them to be strong in the face of enemies," Patala said in a way that curdled her blood. Something foul was coming upon them. In the distant outside, birds began to scream, or at least they sounded like birds in the beginning.

Amba felt the hairs stir on her neck. Blood and belief. And sacrifice. Amba dreaded to think of the price the *gift* would extract from her.

⌘ DOORS ⌘

It was preordained that She would cross paths with the Buffalo-Shaman and then Maha Shamanka. She did not have a choice. She could not escape the fate awaiting Her. She could only be prepared.

But She was a clever one. She soon learned to identify which thought belonged to which realm—Her or Us—and learned to ignore the ones which She got from Us. We had chosen a good vessel this time. Her travails would greatly increase Our knowledge.

When Maha Shamanka threw pollen at Her face— It was hard to describe what happened next. A knowledge broke in the depths of Her–Our blood. It whispered that the strength of the dhyuti-herbs lay in their sap, which could transform any creature into its truest form. And that the personality of the remedy has to match exactly the personality of the imbalance, to be able to mobilise sick life-energy in bodies and correct sick spirits. And that a healant has to be alive for the malevolence to heal. The next few days, it seemed a whole new magical universe opened up for Her–Us.

Knowledge that flew out from Maha Shamanka's mouth lapped upon itself like waves and We gorged on it.

We were hungry for more. She easily summoned phantom crumbs for mice to creep in after making pale minnows leap from the waves; she knew what grew well in the garden and what was left better off in the woods.

"Sickness results from being out of sync with natural spirits."

Maha Shamanka showed Her–Us some secret tricks: how she caught snakes and milked their teeth, coax a drop of venom from the tail of a wasp, heal a dying tree and kill a poison vine with a touch. And what plant seed, in how much amount, made a disturbed mind delirious, and which shrub's oil fevered one's thoughts with phantom pains and what sweet-smelling roots, when powdered, were dangerous for a pregnant lady...which tree's bark in spring was a deadly poison, which leaves in fall were a natural antidote to animal bites...what flower's stamen, when powdered, made one lusty to the point of madness or caused paralysis.

Maha Shamanka was pleased with Our attention and told Us more than intended. Even the forbidden knowledge. About why the product of the same plant could affect a condition, a mood, a thought, a passion, and forbidden salts, the ones She warned Her–Us to stay away from.

"Degree is everything— It decides the healant from poison."

She told Her–Us about the scented pollen-laden flowers of multiple fragrances, whose power waxed and waned with the season, which gave bad dreams and hallucinations in small amounts, and what common flower seeds turned into a deadly poison, strong enough to make a man raving mad, when given in consistent, special doses at timely intervals; about the pollen of multiple fragrances to get demented souls back from the brink, warned Us of the fruit seeds which make peaceful men violent, and brought to light the stamens which healed lust at high moon.

The knowledge was as old as the mountain and wider than the number of herbs found in it. There was no room for error in her brews and concoctions. Fingers would be chafed, muscles strained and eyes stinging, still the drudge wouldn't stop.

Each time it was a mountain to be climbed anew. Searched. Learned. Dried. Chopped. Ground. Cooked. Burnt. Recooked.

Remade. Researched. Every degree of temperature counted. Every grain counted. The ingredients had to be fresh enough, not premature, or the draughts would go stale and rancid. Freshness mattered, she knew from experience, because, at first, all she brewed were mistakes... Draughts which did nothing, pastes which crumbled, some solid dead rocks. Plants, which, when boiled, made a sort of soap; the yew burnt, sending up a choking smog to determine which poppies hid sleep in their veins and which madness, and which hellebore caused death, and how yarrow could close over wounds.

And it could all still fail. Errors, trials, burnt fingers, fetid clouds and coughing fits and stingy, ear-popping draughts. Herbs hid powers in them and it was a gift to be able to draw them out, and there were more who could do it, were masters at it. It was toil and labour. And drudge. It was after years of labour that the herbs gave away their secrets.

The ores wouldn't leap from the mountain, the herbs won't show themselves easily. It was not for the drowsy, the dull, the weak or the coward. It was for Her, the selected one. Constant. Relentless. For She carried the knowledge from last time that it could be done. Her childhood had given Her constant endurance. She would learn to listen to the sap flowing in the plants as well as the blood in Her veins.

Then, it happened. One moment We were bursting with knowledge-gift and the next, without a warning, all of it left Us in a snap.

We were left empty. That once accepted, the gates could not be left swinging wide like a slack mouth leaking mindlessly. The gift had to be protected.

"You are not of the gods who can move as heated water, softening and stretching the rules, because the gods do not care. They don't need to. It's not they who pay the price."

Maha Shamanka's warning was clear and distinct.

18

The night sneaked in as black as velvet tamarind. Thick in a way that would make ordinary people walk closer to each other. Patala had not ventured out of the basement for the last three nights. Her solitary companion, Domovai, guarded her mistress with a near-militant loyalty. But the rapidly dwindling food rations finally forced her to dispatch Domovai to hunt along with her pack, for fresh meat. Soon, an ominous hush descended on Patala's abode.

Vague foreboding made Amba shiver; she could not explain the cold trail of fear which crept around her heart. The purple bruises on her body were turning green at their edges but she felt splintered with ache and a thrum of nameless danger was all around; a debilitating, emotional numbness stuck as fast as glue. Sleep, when it came, was without the usual nightmares. Perhaps the nightmares had passed her by that night. Perhaps she was not on their map that night. Perhaps they were part of her reality now.

She woke in the middle of the night, disoriented and gasping for air. Or it could have been due to the predatory screech of some vengeful bird squawking in a distance. A heavy fog had seeped into her room through the large window left open. It was windy and drizzling and she tried to shut the window, but it jammed and, within minutes, the rain turned vicious and beat with such a violence, the air bubbled into mist and forced her back.

The odd noise came from the direction of the basement.

With a sense that something was off, Amba clambered down the cellar steps. A humongous, primitive iron chimney squatted like a metal god, with monstrous vents flanked by twisting shadows, which snaked all the way down into an ancient furnace. It ended in a massive mantel and bristled with heavy iron andirons and cooking utensils, with one of those huge fires of mixed wood and peat. Even before she entered the ash pit-spot, she could feel soft, black, velvety carbon particles settling on her face, hair and eyes. A brackish smell lay about the incinerator. She did not wish to find out what all had met their blazing ends in this stove.

When she heard the scratching and scrambling about one of the vents, she waited for some small animal to show itself, unless it was trapped. The cellar was so damp that the fire was never allowed to go out, even in midsummer—but, curiously, for the last few days, Patala had left the chimney unfired and it was stone cold.

As she turned to leave, there it was again—a muffled thud, followed by the rustle of cloth and the faint sound of a step carefully laid.

"Hello? Anyone in here?" She called out in a firm voice and immediately felt stupid. Did she expect an animal to start chatting back? Her fingers were becoming stickier and swollen from the briny air, and as she turned back, she slipped badly on some loose stones covered with moss. Her hand shot out for balance and got cut as she fell heavily on her exposed sides. She cried out as stones cut into her skin and pain shot through her wrist.

Coughing to get her breath back, she found it hard to ignore the burning pain on her sides, which now had an open gash. That's when she heard the sound. It was of a mysterious kind—a sound of rustling and of three or four quick beats, like a rapid step. The agony of suspense grew at length and became intolerable and she cautiously moved forward, with her arms extended, and her eyes straining.

A shadow suddenly unfastened itself from the dark and moved towards her. Startled, she choked back a scream. It was Patala.

"Hurry up! Follow me. There is no time!"

Patala's words, barely intelligible, were soft formations carved from her teeth and lips. Her breath could scarcely carry them an inch.

"But who are we hiding from?"

"They are here. The ones you escaped from. I will show you where to hide; they should not find you."

Amba did not need to be told again. Switching on the flashlight, she hurried after the little witch and stepped into what was a dark wetness of a shifting cosmos of shit, crumbling insides of an ancient rotting whale. It was lined by rusting iron sheets and broken asbestos. The flooring was completely broken, with bits of infested wood flooring poking out like crosses in a surreal cemetery. Goblets of greasy, black, oily mud oozed from places, and the tiles wobbled as she walked. For some time, she could not make out if they were going forward or down. The pitted walls transformed to a million faces and spoke of the valleys, mountains, rivers, living and dead they had been a part of in different ages. The contours of ancient ages hidden beneath the old and new. The wall, with its patched and peeling surface, roughened and stained with grime, the process of decay. The door was camouflaged in a way only someone who knew of its existence could find it.

"Why can't you hide with me?" Amba pleaded.

"There is space only for one. Listen to me, girl. Take this with you…my amulet…it will keep you safe." Patala removed her ornament and pressed it into Amba's hands. "The stone is older than the mountains; it is very powerful. Always respect its powers. And this…take it." Amba's eyes widened, for the worn-out leather bag that Patala held out for her contained bullets and a rifle, and a pouch of water to keep her hydrated.

"It has enough rounds. Rusty, perhaps, but they will do the job."

"Let us escape together. You must come with me!" Amba pleaded.

"Where will I run? And why? They can never kill me. Let them find out what's inside of me. Let them find out," Patala rambled in a faint voice, her speech slurred and monotone, like dense fog rolling over life. And the next instant, the door closed on her, the air eating her words.

It was pitch black and Amba crouched low and crawled into the confined space. It reeked of a forlorn smell, intensifying with every breath she took. The dank interiors had swollen the wood and it was hard to peel it off. She used all her strength to beat the dust out, poked bits of a stick into the lock to clear it and peeped out of the keyhole, first with one eye, and then with the other. She was much less disposed to come out than before, and what she saw, horrified her.

The men struck fast.

Quick and precise like lightning.

Several bayonets plunged into Patala's chest.

Noooooo!

Amba clasped her hand to her mouth before she could scream. Nausea rising, hot tears stung her eyes. Patala's wails came as great, awful bouts of sound.

This wasn't happening!

But her desperate thoughts couldn't change the truth. She choked back another scream as the corpse slid to the floor and fell with the crude sound of the dead, heavy like lead, vulgar in its finality. Bile stung fierce; acid and fear smells filled her nose. Quite sobs broke loose as the memory of the blade stabbed again—and again. In her blood, she felt everything again—and again. The earth ripped into half and she vomited out and swallowed, and every sound grew and her skin felt turned inside out.

When Amba came out of hiding, it was almost sunrise. A bitter iron taste coated her mouth and oozed down the back of her throat and she cursed herself for letting her guard down. The house was broken into and looted several times. What marauders could not take, they trashed. The place smelled of urine and the walls were covered with graffiti and the smell of recent violence lingered.

A peculiar and mysterious moaning, like the roar of a hurricane, filled the air. Her senses unmoored, sanity almost deserted her when she stumbled on a body and got saddled in a soggy embrace. She had found Patala. The dreadful quiet was broken by Domovai's wails, as if the soul of the universe was being goaded into mourning, and left her nerves shredded. The beast nudged and prodded her mistress gently—trying to make her get up. But Patala remained still, lifeless as a rock. Massive, jagged lines around her eyes squinted into deep ridges and furrows, her head reared back and tongue rolled forward, with a rasping sound, Domovai lifted her face to the sky and howled.

An eerie answering howl floated down from the dark forest and Domovai lifted her mistress gently in her massive jaws and galloped away with the pack. The apparition, or whatever it might have been, was swallowed by the darkness.

"Where is she? The younger one?" The voice of a man jolted her and she dashed back into her hiding place. The killers had still not left and were looking for her.

"Look around. That bitch would be hiding hereabout. She is crafty, that one. The Colonel wants her alive."

Amba recognised the harsh voice. It was Mathera, who had interrogated her along with Rosie Madbull in the prison.

An abrupt crashing of underbrush was followed by cursing, and she guessed that whoever came, came quickly. There was no time to lose. Her pursuers wouldn't stop till they found her. A sense of running against time filled her up, as did Patala's last words to hurry back to her village.

The sunlight dusted Amba's cut forehead with golden powder and Patala's amulet felt warm against her skin. Holding it between her fingers, she adjusted it around her neck with a cord and touched it to her lips once for luck. Her jacket hung loose, straps floating an inch off her shoulders softened the blow of the ancient and heavy gun each time the bootheel struck hard ground, but at an advantage in the forest, which she knew like the back of her hand, she managed to make quick distance from her pursuers.

A hundred feet from her, the river broke, as it seemed, directly from the base of the cliffs, and in her condition, there was the remotest chance for escape in that direction, so she turned her attention, with great trepidation, towards the forest. The frosty smell of an oncoming blizzard filled her nostrils and it was hard to breathe. The mountain track, bisecting what was wholly Regiment terrain, had proved too violent to build anything lasting. And beyond that, the boggy swamp with a ravine cutting through it and impenetrable jungle on both sides.

She crossed it carefully and proceeded to a ridge where it sheared off the trail, when something whirred past her face at great speed.

19

A sudden rifle round shattered the stone in front of her.

Craaaaaacck!

Amba bent her head against the flying chips and felt a strange electric pain all over her skull, a nerve pain. She couldn't see out of her right eye.

She cupped as much water as she could in her palm, and wiped her eye. It cleared and she was relieved. Then she saw her hand. It glistened red from the blood from her eye.

The blade of stone, blown off the rock by the bullet, had struck her over the right eye and she was thankful it had missed the pupil. The injury was superficial, a surface wound, not as bad as it looked. She must not be incapacitated. Not now. She knew very well what they would do with her if they caught her alive. She was safe for now but the indiscriminate firing by her pursuers had caused a mini-landslide and those below were sprayed by small rocks. Just how many of them were wounded by the flying rocks, she was unsure, but it was a good feeling.

Bending her head, she noticed her knuckles were spotty with red. The eye had clouded again with blood and she used a wet cloth to wipe it off. Luckily it was her right eye, because it was with her left eye that she aimed. The sharp edge of the stone seemed to have hit a nerve, because it was over an hour and the crawling sharp pain all over her scalp not only persisted, but increased manifold. It hurt badly, but at least she could see with both eyes. Her vision was as good as ever. She turned over on her stomach and lay still for over an hour. Enough for them to be eaten with curiosity. She caught a glimpse of a rifle barrel in a notch and smiled as the bullet found its mark.

The sound of lead on flesh was followed by a scream of pain. There was smoke down to the right of the hill. It was definitely a hit. She held her rifle close, feeling grateful for Patala's foresight. She carefully counted the cartridges; they were forty in number. Hoping they would last the day, she clicked out the cylinder and reloaded. She crept forward, watching where she stepped and, feeling thirsty, brought the water pouch to her mouth, rolled onto her back and poured it down. In her haste, some ran down the side of her mouth.

With the forty rounds clattering in her bag, she crawled tight behind the hip of the rock and found her notch. She loaded the cylinder and wasted three more shots, trying to ricochet a round into one of the attackers who was behind the buttress. For a time, she hid behind one of the lesser boulders that were scattered over the top of the hill, but, seeing or hearing nothing for some time, she crept from her place of concealment to undertake a systematic search of her surroundings to make her escape. While she was creeping to her side on her knees, she got a glimpse, over the downward slope, of one of the pursuers. Keeping very still, she peered out from her ambush, waiting to see what he would do. Another man appeared, darting up the ravine and into cover again and caused her to uselessly expend two more shots shots. Was her judgement failing her as well as her strength, she wondered. The only good thing was that she possessed a very good hand despite it all.

Yessss! Another hit!

She was jubilant. But this was no moment to rejoice. It was time to face facts. She flipped open the cylinder of the gun and turned her hand to feel the emptiness with dismay—forty more rounds. She was losing the lead too fast. To make it worse, it was more than seventy-two hours since she had properly rested. The urge to sleep overwhelmed her. To stop would mean a fate worse than death. That overhead sunlight was murder on her skin and almost-unprotected retinas. She squinted her red eyes towards the distant dappled shade of the meadow and was immersed in a flush of longing. Sleep swelled and leaked out of her pores. She wanted to drop her head on her forearm. Just for a moment, if only for a moment, just to get the weight off her head, if only, and she slowly lay her head down. It would be only for a few seconds, she told herself. Her arm was covered with dirt and she wiped it against her chest and lay still. When she lifted it, there was another bloody eye socket imprint on it. She pressed more wet cloth against her eyebrow, followed by strange flashes of pain all over her skull, made worse by the sudden splattering of gunfire.

Amba lunged for cover.

She was left with only eight to ten shots, at the most. Another shot from the left. Wounded or not, the man was shooting, and the smoke told her he had gained higher ground. More than fifty yards away.

If he got above her and started shooting down, she was in big trouble. She opened the bag. It contained shotgun shells.

She reached for it, even as another round smashed into the stone in front of her. She lay back and hefted the shell.

The coins fit perfectly into the paper tube of the twenty-gauge hull. She could not believe her luck! It was very heavy. Amba held the cap and charged it with the powder charger, using her thumb, twenty grains at a time, eighty grains of powder. A heavy load for her shotgun.

She smiled. With the weight of the coins and the powder charge, the shotgun had become something like a small cannon. Not just that, heavy things flew far and fast, so it might give her a range of close to two hundred yards. She stank of cordite and was coated with the black dirt of the valley and her scalp was on fire and the eye was swelling to twice its size. She smiled wide. Perhaps there was a fighting chance of getting out alive now.

Suddenly she found she was no longer tired. First, there were a few ruses and deceptions which had to be accomplished. She took one of the dove shot shells and loaded the old shotgun. With one hand, she laid the barrel in the notch, and with the other, loaded more coins into the shell, and rammed in the wads with a stick, poured out the powder from the old spring-loaded charger, rammed in another wad and finally twisted each hull firmly shut. Amba fired down the ravine and heard the light beads of the seven dove tinkle harmlessly on the stone.

Not from far below, a familiar voice called out, "Witch, is that all you got?"

"Come on closer, dog. You will find out," she shouted back.

"I am scared now. You are shooting cake decorations at me!" Mathera mocked. "She is shooting pebbles. Next, she will throw her shoes."

"Well, come on then, bastard, why don't you find out? Maybe you are right, maybe you are wrong," Amba retorted.

"We intend to find out. And, bitch, you won't be happy with the way we do the finding!" His voice was loaded with murderous intent.

"I will find out then, dog, won't I? Why are you scared? Why are you hiding?" she shouted, hoping he would fall and bleed to death. She wondered how long they would take to come up and loaded another round and fired. It sprayed out its tiny beads into the air like poppy seeds.

"Come on, girl. Let's make a deal," Mathera shouted again.

He doesn't need to make a deal, she thought, he is probably thinking everything is on his side. He just wants to kill her—she thought—take a souvenir—maybe her head—as proof of her death to Madbull.

The call came again. She should not heed. They were deceitful.

What did they take her for? She was angry. Perhaps they thought of her as foolish, green behind the ears. She could not trust the crafty bastards. They would take her alive and kill her in front of the villagers, to terrify them enough to abandon the land and leave. She needed to stop thinking.

She worked the bolt and the old hull jumped out, smoking, and she grabbed it. Now she slipped one of her coins / dime shells into the breech. The weight of it should give her a good hundred and seventy yards, if not more. She laid a barrel into the notch.

"So, what's your deal?" she asked.

"I will be reasonable," Mathera's voice echoed.

"Come up and talk, then. Why so slow?"

"You don't have any malicious intent? You won't shoot me in the head?"

"Stop being a coward," Amba taunted.

"Do we have a deal?" Mathera chuckled.

"Problem is you keeping the deal."

Silence.

Why was he delaying? She knew the only reason could be to keep her talking while his associate crept up on her.

Far to her left, a small trickle of sand and rocks spilled down the ravine.

Mathera confidently walked out from behind the buttress of stone, taking irregular short and long steps with his strong mountain legs. Probably, he was guessing the range of her firearm, and perhaps thought she was out of ammo.

"Witch, you think you can outrun my bullet? You think your bones can stop my bullet. The body can take only so much of a ripple. Not equipped to take a wave. Not for girls who pretend to be witches!"

"Thank you for the free class. Your dogs need it more, from the looks of it."

"She has a mouth, hasn't she…! Witch has some mouth on her!"

"Your men should be grateful they are still alive and in one piece. Now, they can keep coming after me. But the situation will not change. Only they, and you, will get more and more tired. And you know what is the terrible part? That they would give a limb or two to be in the same scared, shitless situation tomorrow, and the day after, for it will mean they are alive."

"If you are not scared, why are you hiding from us cowards, then? You know what I think? You are not shooting enough and now you are scared, and in your desperation, you have reverted to the shotgun and its pepper-light loads."

She did not say anything. Instead, she advanced up the ravine as swift as a mountain goat, her body dark and red with sweat and heat.

"I tell you what. You put down that shotgun and I will make sure my men empty their magazines, and we can have a conversation."

Two hundred yards.

Come closer.

A little bit closer.

"I am putting it down as we speak."

Come on, come closer, you bastard.

She aimed very carefully. She wasn't sure what the coins would do or the extra heavy powder charge. So, she aimed for the 'V' of the advancing man's open shirt collar and pulled the trigger. The dimes roared out of the muzzle at eight hundred feet per second with a three-feet long muzzle blast. The gun smoke expanded in a great thick cloud and the stock slammed back into her shoulder, almost hard enough to dislocate it.

It was Manimal. Probably sent by Mathera at the last moment, she thought. The load hit him squarely on the forehead. As the dimes flew out, they turned on edges, so that when they impacted his forehead, it looked as if his head was suddenly imprinted with bloody red hyphens. The hyphens imprinted on his chest were drooling thick blood. An expression of complete shock was frozen on his face as he fell backwards, his head downhill. The last she saw of him was his boot soles rapidly disappearing down the rocky slope. She jerked off the wet cloth and shoved it in between the butt of the stock and her shoulder. And then, without turning her head, she shoved another dime-loaded shotgun shell, slapped it in, shot the bolt home, brought the sights to bear on Mathera, scrambling away as fast as he could from his dead master as he could. Another bellow and coins hissed through the air, faster than sight, and they sparkled and ricocheted all the way down the ravine.

The roar of the overloaded twenty-gauge sounded like a grenade had gone off. Flying metal discs pierced Mathera's backside and he roared in pain and fear. A shower of little discs tore through the trees lower down and clipped branches and leaves of the live oak, spanged off stone, gained momentum, almost chipped the skin off Mathera's skull. He turned around to fight and she unloaded on him again. It was too close and the load sliced him sideways and he crumpled senseless from the impact.

When he came to, trapped between two boulders, his leather belt, torn off his person, bound him such that he could not move even if he tried. Mathera spat and cursed her and she slapped his face several times, till his mouth leaked blood. Mathera's eyes flickered with fear at that. Amba finally leaned back, her nerves glowing with charge, and smiled. And then she gave in to the bubble of laughter which rose from her stomach and laughed and laughed till she sucked in air and tears streamed down her face. She turned and warmed her hands over the small fire. She left Mathera to work on the rawhide thongs that bound his wrists. He had plenty to work on with his teeth, she told him. His teeth had rot set in them. And that was the point. She could hear him try to chew of the cords. Ever so often she heard him curse and spit, a tooth at a time. She panicked him into chewing till he was all gum. Never again would you bite into a *Habishi* buffalo. Or a Hori woman, she said.

She was not done with him. An outgrowth of the red mountain shrub, known for its deadly roots, had caught her attention when she was dragging him, still unconscious, and now she planned to make him helpless altogether. Mathera, exhausted from his efforts, finally slept and she got her chance to carefully dab the shrub's poison roots, its toxins leaching slowly, into his eyes. He would never shoot straight now. That is, if he ever escaped the snakes and centipedes, she said, and his eyes widened in panic. Grey, unkept, skin gone sallow. His voice a murmur. He was lachrymose with pain, his face bathed with sweat, mucus, vomit and tears. The painful droop of his shoulders and the sweating fingers indicated he would not hold his side in a fight for long.

"Half the *Habishis* hate you so much, they are going to stake you down, buck naked, and skin you alive." Amba was surprised when he smirked.

"Too late for that, isn't it!"

"What do you mean?"

"Now you are asking me questions? Why should I answer you?" His voice sounded as dull as a ruined blade.

"Because if you don't, I will slash you with my knife and the vultures, who nest nearby, will have a taste of your blood and flesh while you live."

"No, you will not."

With a mean swipe of the sharp dagger, she ripped through his arm, spilling fresh blood, and Mathera screamed in pain.

"Witch! I hope you die! Wiiiitch!"

She had to make things quite unpleasant before Mathera revealed what he knew. It was not much help though. All he knew was that Madbull had sent all the regular officers on leave; only the Red-Hounds were carrying out his orders. And that they were loading lots of fuel and ammunition in trucks.

Amba wasn't tired anymore. Her eye and skull were still on fire. She lay down and allowed herself to breathe slowly. Frayed, dirty nerves humming as telegraph wires in wind, she climbed over the lip of the rock. In a little while, she would be close to collapse. She must make it to the bottom in one piece, she told herself, before the deluge came, which would make any movement slippery and lethal. The air reeked of cordite and sulphur and gave her a headache. So did the whispering inside her ears, now a constant thrum she found more and more difficult to ignore; the innumerable lacerations from the stinging nettle marked her face and back and legs, and the rain burned through, setting each cut on fire.

Somewhere close by, Madbull's men were still hunting for her, but as she looked up and caught the sun's light, refracting and cutting the heavens into a complicated geometry of ice and air and fire, she wondered if Patala was watching her right now. The only solid thing which anchored her to reality was the hard thud of the rifle against her shoulder. Time didn't seem to run forwards anymore, it was a solid thing you could press back against and feel it push back, a thick fluid, part solid, part gas, part glass, that flowed both ways between old recollections and new sensations. And, in the middle of the new sensations, Patala seemed to warn her to never let her witch slip out and self-hunt.

⌘ BINDING ⌘

The prophecies would come later. The shifting, the skinnings and the re-shapings, the falling and the revival of scales.

We watched from inside—breathing, floating, pulsating. Preparing.

She understood it was useless to try to deny Us. She understood it was impossible to remain a singular entity.

She had finally accepted that We were not going anywhere. She stopped fighting Us. Soon, She did not mind Us. In a way, it was just being on a new track. She was moving smoothly through the doors. She would be better prepared for the re-birthing.

She always was a terrifyingly beautiful thing. We had only seen Her at a fraction of Her fullest. Heavy with power yet unbearably light. She would have to learn this new balance between Her and Us.

She would have to unlearn and shed Her human ways, soon.

20

War or worse, there was terror afoot and Tanu Bakar was sure of it as sweat after nerves. Under this shadow of fear, his 'slaughter with slaughter' call against the Red-Hounds had fizzled down to a helpless appeal, impotent in its anguish. Last night, under the cover of darkness, he managed to sneak past any lurking Red-Hounds, into the village. The savagery of the attack left him shaken. Flames and smoke poured out of holes blasted through walls of homes. Incessant rains had turned streets into slurries of water bloated with blood and flesh. The villagers looked haunted; exhausted from sweeping out rotting corpses of dead animals, which clogged the bloated drains. His optimism of having escaped from the Red-Hounds was replaced with foreboding. Intense grief scourged his heart when he heard how Sushithal met his end, but he knew worse was to come. Tanu Bakar knew the villagers blamed him for not being there to protect them. For a blazing moment, he was consumed with the thought of giving himself up—surrendering to Madbull, ending the insanity—but the thought was abandoned almost instantly. Surrendering would not make any difference. Madbull wanted to exterminate the *Habishis*, to get to the gold he believed was buried under their soil. He would never stop.

Hiding in the caves with his men seemed the only way out; if only so they could live to fight another day. But he was not so sure as he looked at the haunted faces. The men were weary and tense, their whispers muffled by dread stained their faces. Hunger, made worse by the bitter cold and rains, had started reflecting upon everyone's frames, and they made the kind of noises made by those who lived in darkness and misery. Tanu Bakar desperately missed Amba; his strong and brave Amba would have *known* what to do. He was not sure if she was even alive, or if he would get to see her again, and the thought was a punch in the gut.

This lot in front of him was in no condition to take on the savage Red-Hounds with their overwhelming numbers and extreme brutality. He felt hopeless. For any human being, great suffering comes from losing land, but the suffering is greatest from losing hope. Not just hope, it felt as if he was losing skin off his face.

Last night, he had a horrible presentiment that they would all starve together and freeze to death. To fight the brutal cold, men were torching anything that would burn, for a moment's heat. Wrapped in rags, bundled in pieces of worn clothing too big for them, or too small, paper stuffed into jackets and pants, the men huddled close to each other. Provisions were exhausted. And they had taken to killing rats and other vermin. The pile of little bones on their plates, sucked clean of every bit of meat and tendon. Regardless of what it was, they still longed for another serving. The rats were field mice and the bats, black mice. It hardly mattered. *Meat is meat, we eat what we must*, he heard them whisper all night.

"Tara and the women are safe, you say, but for how long? Even if Madbull's men spared some women this time, they will be back, and then who knows what will happen? I should never have left her alone. I must go back," Nakul said.

"You would be of no use to her dead."

"I am also no use to her hiding in the caves like a coward. I have decided. I will try to survive the bullets when they come."

"That's foolish. Madbull's men are looking for us like packs of mad dogs…They will stop at nothing. And if they catch you, you will get them to us," said one of the men, looking downcast, and a host of voices erupted, whimpering for their families.

"We are all doomed! Our families will starve and die in the cold," wailed Rodh. "I have heard our people are dying like rats. Fighting over handfuls of food. All supplies are either gone or destroyed. The weather will become worse, and those remaining will freeze."

"Enough. Keep quiet all of you!" commanded Tanu Bakar. "Let's not lose our heads. Keep all your warm clothes. Ration your food carefully. We must regain our strength, our spirits."

"But, by then, all that's worth saving could be lost!" said Nakul. "You sound like a farmer begging god not to send swarms of locusts into his fields before harvest time. Soon we will crawl on all fours. I will go back and try to save what little is left…I should never have left…Maybe Tara will forgive me…" Nakul said despairingly.

"What do you suggest then? That we fight them? What will we fight them with? Brass cannon and iron shot, rammers and charging ladles, serpentine powder and brimstone, five hundred yew bows and ten barrels of bowstrings, two hundred each of spades, shovels, crowbars, pickaxes, horsehides, two hundred felling axes, one thousand horse shoes, ten thousand nails?" Tanu Bakar raged, and it lent his face a hollow, rapacious intensity. He could not bear being hemmed in by all those breathing, anxious bodies and incessant talk of defeat. "Misery has stalked us since we lost Amba. I wish she would come back."

"The witch will save her kind. What use she has of us?"

"Don't look at me like that!" Nakul said, noticing Bakar's frown. "You need her only because we want to use her strength, now that we are weak. She will be stupid to risk her life and come back to save us. She should, as much, damn all of us to hell!"

Nakul's words were left hanging in the air like a loaded gun, not fired yet, but its impact pulsated down to Tanu Bakar's bones.

"I should never have come. I should have known there would be no hero here but a bunch of cowards—cowards who hide when they should protect."

"Cowards? Us? Coming from a man like you—"

"I never claimed to be a hero. I don't have any pretensions. I am not the problem here. They want you, Master Bakar. Why don't you give yourself up and give our families, the ones still alive, a chance?"

"Giving myself up will not serve any purpose. They will take me and still do what they want to do. Even if he has both me and Amba, Madbull won't be content till his goal is achieved." Tanu Bakar's voice was gruff.

"So, you would rather let more of us die, if it calms them, if it slows them down, and you live a day more?" hissed Nakul. The men, who would not have their leader thus disrespected, charged towards him but Tanu Bakar raised his hand to stop them.

There was a time when Tanu Bakar thought Nakul was the most beautiful boy he had ever seen. Despite the age difference, he had fallen hopelessly in love. In love with his soft, golden hair, skin like a magnolia petal, hair as black as a raven's wing and deepest-brown eyes. To him, Nakul looked like a delicate china ornament. In spite of himself, the memory of that emotion brought hot tears that stung his eyes. He still longed to touch him, to brush his hand against his perfectly shaped cheekbones, and under the feathers of his thick, dark lashes. But that time was long gone. And, lately, Tanu Bakar had realised that what they had shared once and the real Nakul were not one and the same. The fact dawned upon him slowly that Nakul's interest had changed into strongest revulsion and remorse. Not only was Nakul treating him with contempt, he enjoyed playing with him, like a cat with a mouse. There was an underlying threat to his words, replete with warning—*I can tarnish that noble and pure image you so proudly portray*. Like a sudden dagger drawn from its sheath, the swift thrust of half-formed words—and the unsaid threat—*I can expose you if I want to.*

It was clear to him that Nakul had become so hardened in his conscience that he would not care about the consequences of his actions. He shuddered to think what would happen if the men got to know about their relationship. Not only would they never accept his leadership but his hard-earned legacy would also be in shambles. Tanu Bakar pressed his forehead to the weather-beaten skin of his arm. In his nervous state, he imagined Nakul smiling and taunting him—*Are you scared? How does that feel? Get used to it*. Nakul had always felt pressure more acutely than others and was becoming more volatile by the day.

There was no telling what Nakul would do next. Tanu Bakar was sure he did not want to leave his fate at the mercy of a man whose passions were so revengeful. If he let himself be weak now, it was going to extract a high toll from him, and that could not be allowed to happen.

The implied threat in Nakul's words was not lost on him.

Nakul sat on the stone slab, a few feet from the sheer drop, shivering, as if summoning the guts, which had deserted him again. The land around was rutted by lattices of gullies and bogs, all of them bearing stones and gravel down from the Hori mountains, and the night wind, with its presentiment of winter, cut cold lashes on his face. He knew he could not go back. Not after he had glimpsed the contempt on Tara's face. The river down below, bathed in a misty shroud, beckoned him softly, and he wondered if he should end it. End it all. He stared down the bottom winding into the mist. An unexpected noise set his heart racing and he turned around in panic. Tanu Bakar was walking towards him.

"You! Are you following me? Why don't you leave me alone?" Nakul asked angrily.

"Your behaviour disturbs me. We have to talk."

"Don't come near me—keep away!"

"Nakul, I know what you were doing there. What were you trying to achieve by threatening me? It cannot be that you don't know how much this loathing in your very attitude hurts me. To see the hate and the revulsion that surges through your heart, to guess the hard, cold thoughts, which fill your mind against me because we loved once. I feel betrayed."

Nakul exclaimed, and with an expression of disgust about his mouth, he spat.

"You are not fit to lead." The air bristled with his words.

"What have I done to deserve this unjust treatment? You feel I have used you? Have *I* not been used? I remain what I am, and you have punished me enough by withdrawing your friendship entirely from me. But can we not be kind, can we not—"

"Don't speak. Shut up. Shut up." Nakul stamped his feet, and his rage grew until the muscles of his face worked into a fury, and his fingers clenched until his nails bit into his flesh. Such was the bitterness in his tone that Tanu Bakar stepped back, staring at him with a haunted look. Also, because he had a feeling that they were no longer alone.

21

Feverish from pain in her eye, Amba fell in an exhausting stupor. The day was hotter than a witch's womb and Amba wanted to shed her flesh and sit in her bones. This was remote land, rocky and thickly wooded, with none of the quaint appeal of rolling hills. History and struggle had sanctified many a spot, valley, stream and tree here.

It wasn't clear to her whether she walked that night or whether she simply hung on to a beast bucking and heaving under her. Sweat gushed out of her in heaps, harsh and feral. Plucking off leeches, stuck like stubborn memories to the exposed parts of her body, she trudged for long hours through the Jotsoma forest's treacherous undergrowth. Her neck trapped sweat and frothed into an abrasive paste and patches of skin behind her ears seemed to rub away. A bizarre debris of green, in different stages of decay, an exotic dispensation of pale amaranth and tall poplars and fennels, the cornels shrivelling on their fruits, dwarfed her with their spindly arms in a conspiring huddle fifty feet above her. The air, atrophied and faintly rotten, struck her senses at all levels. The temperature dropped at dusk due to passage of thick rain clouds, the atmosphere now a dense liquid. She bent her head back to look up into the leafy canopy and the rain-bloated sky. Water drops soon cascaded from the spidery hands of giant trees. It was a wet world, where each leaf of every tree, clinging to the twigs throughout the winter, held a drop at its tip.

A change in the wind's direction brought welcome relief. Then, the temperature plunged and it became dark, though it was nearly five. A freak hailstorm plunged her into a hellish twilight of morbid white and grey dust, followed by a near-apocalyptical cloudburst and winds howling at fifty miles per hour. The good part, it turned out, was that the cold rain had begun to revive her. Amba finally allowed herself to think about Nakul, and despite herself, succumbed to a tide of dismaying emotions as she recalled how he had abandoned her and ran off like a coward. She had to face the fact that he was too gutless to do what he must have known to be right, or indeed too cowardly to avoid doing what he knew to be wrong. But, was his character, or the lack of it, a complete surprise, she asked herself. Besides, their bond stood broken for far too long. She always knew that Nakul had sublimated all the grief he must have felt for their mother, who he worshipped, into anger for her, his sister, who he hated.

He had worsened after their mother's rape, and his meanness towards her was more disturbing than any of his outbursts. When Tanu Bakar adopted them, Nakul's erratic mood swings and temper tantrums subsided and were replaced by something else, something more permanent, and hard. When she would return from school during the holidays, she would inevitably find him sitting in silence, his face to the wall, disoriented; his eyes shining with a strange shame; a baffling darkness from which she was forever excluded. Over time, she had learned to simply play along for as long as she could, in only the most perfunctory way, till their bond became mechanical and forced. Nakul's betrayal did not surprise her, since there were no expectations, yet, it was not going to be easy to forgive him, she told herself.

The valley below lay veiled and mysterious, silent in the foggy night. She knew some Regiment men kept houses in different parts of the Hori, with exteriors left deliberately shabby and uncared for so that they blended into the general squalor. And that, if taken this time, there would be no mercy. Abandoned houses shone with contours of ages too soiled to touch. Broken household utensils and tribal totems placed at various nooks and crannies to placate annoyed spirits. Cutting south across the west arterial road, and from a point onwards, the mountain road got crammed and houses smaller, and more and more roofs were just zinc sheets held down with bricks. The trenches were intersected by canals groves, perfect if an enemy was looking to hide. At several points, the road bisected into what was wholly Regiment terrain. Incessant rains and the brutal cold had discouraged all except the most urgent business and the streets were empty. A few bedraggled men hunched under awnings, huddled together in a tight group to ward off the icy cold with an air of grim surrender, unmoving in the torn muck of the road. As she strode by, none showed even a flicker of interest in the drugged slack of their eyes. Three miles down, a stretch of the confusing geography, she stepped into Hori at night—a habitation of bleak and unremitting ugliness. By the time she approached the hills bordering her village, the moon had set, but the night was so transparent that the white house-fronts between the trees looked grey against the snow. Clumps of bushes made black stains on them and the moon sent shafts of insipid light far across the endless undulations.

The loud crack of a branch startled her. Her right hand unconsciously reached for the pistol in her waistband, tightening her grip. The underbush rustled and a dim shape emerged from behind a thick cluster of fennels. Her heart raced, because despite the distance, the figure, bathed in cold mist, looked oddly familiar. The man simply sat there, his back to the cliff wall. There was no sense of tension or urgency in him; there was nothing about his body which suggested violence. The distance was still too large to get a good look at his face though. A ragged plume of smoke directed her gaze towards a cave against the piling. She crossed a little bridge across a dry ravine and hid near the cave to get a better view.

Her initial sentiment was a surge of pity—the same sort of emotion evoked when one sees an abandoned soul, influenced by opiates not distinguishable from dark squalor of the bare tenements. She relaxed the tension in her fingers and took her hand from the firearm and quietly released the breath that she was holding in.

The man's forlorn face was picked out by the slowly emerging lights against the dark dusk.

Nakul!

It was Nakul. Her heart now thumped against her ribcage.

How was that possible? Things don't work out like that! It was, at first, incomprehensible. But now that the providential occurrence was apparent, she hardly knew whether to laugh at its sheer absurdity or censure its impertinence. Perhaps an obscure part of her had wished for half a miracle as such, for want of strength to believe in a whole one. It was not a hallucination. The absurdity of the moment was so apparent that it could only be happening for real, she told herself, and smiled. But the look on Nakul's face stopped her.

It was ashen, like a soul in purgatory. He raised his hands as he looked up and shouted out at the heavens above, imploring for clemency. And the skies scowled back, watching the passage of the mortal.

Approaching noiselessly, for a moment, she regarded him silently. He seemed to be living in a world completely his own, and in the small motions of his face, the brow raised or lowered, the eyes narrow or widened, the lips set and reset, and the play of his hands, she saw him progress from phase to phase of his own truth/story spinning out inside him. Once he clenched his fist and leaned forward, once it brought into his face an expression of torment and despair—when this passed, its stamp lingered in his eyes.

She was about to call out to him when she noticed he was not alone. He was in animated conversation with another man and she noticed it was none other than Tanu Bakar!

A soft warmth invaded her and she felt a strong desire to run and hug both the men, but instinct told her otherwise. Something warned her to not to reveal herself yet, perhaps because the postures of the two men did not suggest it was a friendly meeting. Amba moved closer to a spot where she could hear what they were saying, without being spotted.

"You should not have threatened me," Tanu Bakar was saying forlornly.

"A sinner like you will not tell me what to do. You don't deserve respect from people. When they know your truth, they will hate you." He stomped his foot upon the ground and scowled.

A wild trembling seized her and she released the breath she was holding back, as though her eyes had opened on a sordid secret.

"It was in the past. So long ago…Can't you find it in your heart to forgive me, Nakul?"

"Don't take my name with your sinful mouth. There will be no absolution, no mercy for your crimes. You must pay—

for what you did to me, to the other boys—" Nakul's voice was shaking with anger.

Amba hugged herself to stop the shivering. She was scared of the nature of the truth which was emerging. Giant phantoms continued to cover the truth with their big fists and she struggled to hear against the wind, which had changed direction.

"You cannot blame me. I only loved you. As you did me."

"Shame! Shame, that you call that lust of an animal, love! Made me an animal too! Shame, that you put in words your perverse acts."

"You will dishonour me in front of everyone? I will be finished. Once I show my weakness, once I do that, the men would lose respect for me. Would refuse to acknowledge me. All the medals in the world won't get me that again. Once the men get to know, you might as well as write 'dead' on my forehead. Is that your wish?"

"Love? Respect? You try to act noble when you are but a pervert with a sick mind."

"I only loved you from the moment I saw you. Our love was never for flesh, but for blood, for kinship—"

Tanu Bakar's countenance became piteous. Nakul pushed him back. Grief had made him slovenly and his punch missed its mark and he crumpled on the floor in an awkward heap. Tanu Bakar moved to help. But Nakul slapped away his hand and looked away in disgust.

"*Our* love? I am not like you! You are sinful and I hope you die a lonely death. Away from your darling Amba. The sicko and the witch—what a pair you both make."

"You condemn and discard one who has not deserved such treatment, without giving a reason or a chance to explain. You might hate me and you might revile me, and heap indignity after indignity upon me, as you have, but the fact remains that I loved you, and I still do—!"

The words planted themselves in a crude fashion, right in front of her eyes, turning round and round in the air, taunting her, and if she tried to ignore, the sharp-edged question made little jabs on her skin and drew blood.

A dense cloud formed in the centre of Amba's chest, changing the rhythm of her beating, making it harder every second as she grasped the true nature of Nakul's hatred. Bile rushed up her throat. All that time, all those years. She couldn't breathe, thinking of when, during brief visits, she would find him pale, withdrawn and then increasingly aggressive, and how alone he must have been, how helpless and baffled, and anguished fury became fine dust that mixed with her blood and coursed through her veins. Despite the voluminous darkness, it was like the lifting of a burden and the unblinding of the eyes.

Tanu Bakar did not see Amba till she was right behind him. Consumed with shame, he suddenly seemed to have trouble breathing and all colour left his face; his body sagged and, eyes bulging, he backed away, stumbled and fell.

22

Tanu Bakar's countenance was flushed with shame. He lowered his eyes, refusing to meet Amba's gaze.

"Amba—It is you! I thought I was dreaming!" He moved weakly to hug her but she pushed him away. He sat down with a thump, all the energy gone out of his legs; he looked pale and shattered.

"Don't turn away from me, Amba! I have always treated you like my daughter. You have to believe me. I never ever intended to harm him..." Tanu Bakar lamented. "I am sorry. Sorry—don't look at me like that, Amba!" he said over and over again. Like a fish gasping for air, he opened his mouth to say something more, then collapsed, his carefully constructed facade melting. A scathing silence emanated from Amba as she struggled to come to terms with the damning revelations. Bakar quivered under her scrutiny.

Nakul's eyes locked with Amba's, and, for a brief moment, they lost connection with all things around, swallowed by a tsunami of emotions. He saw the knowledge of his shame in her eyes and looked away.

"This is not your matter. Go away."

"Nakul, please listen to me."

"Get away! Go!"

"I did not know. He betrayed both of us, Nakul."

"There is no both of us! It happened to *me*. You did not spend your nights in fear and days in shame. How dare you equate what happened to me with you?"

"I will never do that. I suffered, too…my brother."

For almost the first time in her life, she felt truly sorry for Nakul and almost forgot the danger she was in. Most of all, she wanted him to know how much she loved him, but now it seemed she was walking over a battlefield. She walked to him and put her arm around his shoulder. "Don't be sad," she said.

He looked up coldly at her.

"Don't touch me!" he lashed out against the pity in her eyes for his ignoble destiny. Confused, she moved back a step away from him. Amba looked at her brother with her cold, green eyes. Her face was hard and lovely and pitiful. She spoke thoughtfully and deliberately.

"I am sorry. I was just thinking—" she began, but Nakul stopped her.

"I don't want to hear it."

"Don't feel ashamed. You did nothing wrong, Nakul. I understand—"

"Damn you! Why did you even come here? To save me from myself?" he taunted.

"No. You have to give me a chance to speak."

"Strong sister saving her cowardly brother who left her at the mercy of the enemy. I would rather have you tell me to my face that I am not a man, that I am a coward. But, no, you have to be the kind one. I am sick of you. If I need any saving at all, it is from you—your contamination."

Contamination.

Her heart wept with anger and hurt at the abuse but her face remained expressionless, though her eyes got colder. *Contamination*. His word for her rang in her ears, tore her insides from within, and she let it.

"You think I am a contamination?"

"Aren't you? Don't you contaminate everything you touch?"

"That's a wretched thing to say."

"Why? Just because you don't say it, don't I know what you think of me? What they all think of me but dare not say to my face because they are scared of you! You think I am a coward. I see it in your eyes. I see the pity for me. Don't bother wasting your emotion now. It's too late for that. For I only have contempt for you. For all of you."

Tanu Bakar's wretched voice waded in, "Amba, talk to me. Don't turn away, Amba!" He sounded weak, and the air about him was misshapen, as if too weak to hold the weight of its own womb. Noticing the gun in his hand, she decided to exercise caution.

"I never harmed him, Amba. You shall never see me again. But if I have ever done right by you, remember that just as justice is the deepest thing inside you—forgiveness is the other deepest th—"

Braaaaaaaaakkkkkkkkkkkkkkk!!!

A sudden flash of light and sound blinded and deafened them. Earth and gravel pelted her and she flinched. Nakul was on his stomach. She huddled on the ground, arms over her head and shook off the earth that was lining her face.

Tanu Bakar lay on the ground, writhing in pain. There was a gaping hole where his leg was supposed to be. It was obvious there was nothing anyone could do to help him.

"His leg is gone!" Nakul gasped out the words. Bakar was screaming in agony, pointing with demented eyes at the bloody stump that remained of his leg.

"Will he make it?" she asked Nakul. His answer was lost in Tanu Bakar's mind-numbing moans and then more screams, which seemed to swell and fill the entire universe.

"Nonooo...nooo...god...o mercy...nooo...god...no... god...ahhh—"

"Shut him up, Nakul," Amba muttered. "The whole valley will be hearing this."

Nakul looked shell-shocked with disbelief.

"Nakul! Hold him down!" she repeated, but Nakul was frozen. Tanu Bakar's heart-rending wails became shriller.

"Nakul, either you do it or I do it alone, and that would make it more painful for him."

Low, animal moans emanated from his mouth. The molar of the bone protruded above the knee and Nakul tied a pointless tourniquet on his gaping red stump. Amba put her hand on Tanu Bakar's mouth, muffling his loud screams and with the other hand, squeezed shut his nostrils.

Gradually the thrashing and the strangled moans ceased and, at last, he was still. A part of her wondered if Tanu Bakar was really dead because she kept hearing his screams in her head.

"We have to move now. There is no time—Listen! Pay attention! There is no time for this...We have to get out!"

"We should bury him," Nakul replied dully.

"No," she said. "They must have heard his screams. They will come when there is light." Nakul bowed next to Tanu Bakar's corpse in a gesture of praying.

"We have to move now. We have to leave him here—"

"No, no, I cannot. I cannot leave him like this! He loved me and that was his only crime. I should hate him, but I can't. I cannot bring myself to hate him—*he* loved me—" Nakul said, his voice hoarse with grief. "I cannot leave him in such a condition."

Nakul was sitting, his head bowed over his silent gun, some twenty metres away. A puff of concrete dust rose when a shrapnel pinged off again and a red heart slowly expanded on his white shirt. Her mouth dry, Amba tossed her rucksack and ran straight and fast towards them. Nakul was making guttural noises.

"We cannot leave him here!"

"Brother, we cannot do anything for him now. Let us go."

But Nakul refused to move. She shook him forcefully so he would loosen his grip on Bakar's corpse. With one tug, she prised the dead body from his arms, and as she did so, the body tumbled on to the road.

"Okay. I think you are right," she conceded. "Let's not waste time, then. We have to go as far away from here as possible before morning."

The leg lay served on a bed of shredded ferns, meat tattered and strips of black cloth still clinging to the mangled, white bone. Bits of pink flesh and skin and tissue hung on to the ferns already crawling with ants. Nothing went to waste. She carried the leg with one hand, her other hand on the strap of the rifle, which hung from her shoulder. The burden of carrying the leg seemed far heavier than carrying a whole man. She set down Tanu Bakar's severed leg and dug a shallow grave. Her hands were gummy with blood and she knelt by the creek to wash them in cold water. Nakul unrolled the coat, which was mostly intact, and put the leg inside.

In the pink light, she saw Tanu Bakar's slack mouth and eyes frozen with the shock of sudden death. As Nakul was wrapping the body in the cape, the leg slipped out. There was nothing to do, so she picked up the leg and tucked it in. They dragged the body to near the mouth of the cave, where the air hung wet and cold. They moved slowly and tentatively towards the nearest hole and she slid her hands along the slick ridges. Within minutes, and even as she helped scoop mud to fill the grave, glistening worms were already wriggling out of the soil, attracted by the smell of the fresh blood, ready to feast.

She dug the hole deep, to cover their tracks long enough till the animals smelled it out and dug up the corpse and ate it. Hopefully, the enemies would be left clueless by a disgusting, unidentifiable mess of flesh and bones. In the forest, the story did not end with death. The entire forest was alive with the antics of death and to live in the forest was to be perpetually haunted by the inevitability of one's own decay. Night came and the forest went unnaturally quiet. Uneasy, Amba stared down the length of her weapon and gazed into the dark—for they were in wholly Regiment area. They were both very tense. And alone. Except, perhaps, human ghosts and beast ghosts and plant and insect ghosts, and ghosts of dead tigers and bats and snakes and every little bit of the dead, haunted by the memories of life, claiming a space in the afterlife as well.

The next hour, they managed to reach a secluded spot on the upper bank of the Iravati river, undiscovered. Nakul continued to look shaken, but Amba hoped it would pass with time. It struck her, how weird both them looked in their capes of leaves, their faces splattered with black soil. Nakul showed signs of recovery when he suggested constructing a small raft of bamboo trunks strapped together. They could row themselves across the river with makeshift paddles made of bamboo. As Nakul hurriedly put together a raft, Amba lay guard on the river bank, huddled under her cape of leaves, her back to the river and weapon aimed at the dark forest, from where danger could jump out any moment.

The 'boat', a basic open craft, when ready, at best looked a risky proposition. Faced with no other option, Nakul got in to test it, but the waters were strong and kept butting into the boat, as if challenging the new inhabitant. Amba clutched her rifle and was about to board, but the next instant, she watched in horror as the boat turned turtle and became unmanageable. Nakul disappeared under the boat, which lay inverted. But he was a good swimmer; she told herself; he would not drown, she told herself. The Iravati, however, was at high tide, and even good swimmers could find it difficult to breach the current, but she drove that thought out.

The sudden noise of guns going off pierced the quiet. She threw herself flat on the ground, the short blasts hammering her ears. She struggled to manoeuvre into position but the soreness of her knees and the weight of her weapon made it tough. When she squeezed the trigger, the ancient gun kicked her in the shoulder. The muzzle flash shone bright in the pitch-black night and anyone who was trying to kill them, for sure, knew her exact position. The only thing to do now was keep the attack mode on, keep the attention on herself so Nakul would have time to swim back to safety. Her shoulder felt bruised and broken from the constant kicking of the gun, and when she paused to eject a magazine and load the next, her ears, subjected to the stereophonic effects of the ambush, felt torn out of their sockets. The woods filtered men and the fields became dotted with curving fronts, which bristled and flashed with angry firings. Fireballs. Hundreds of them. Madly flickering on and off in the forest in an insane dance. Only, they were muzzle flashes. To shoot back, she would have to lift her head and take aim but the bullets were flying too close. Miraculously, the shooting stopped and silence descended on the hills. Nakul was back safe and sound and they were still planning their next move when she saw the vehicle. Still a speck, it cut across the terrain and headed straight towards them.

"It's the Red-Hounds! Run, Amba! They have seen us!" Without pausing in his stride, Nakul shouted, pointing at the approaching van.

"Get down, Nakul! They are getting ready to fire—"

"Stop, stop! What are they screaming!" He pointed at the vehicle rushing frantically, turning and twisting its course, as if in a game of tag with some invisible playfellows.

"Shoot, shoot— No— No, wait!"

"Waving! He is waving! Is he friendly? Why is he waving?"

"I don't know! I can't identify him from here!"

"It's a trap! Shoot him down! It's a trap!"

Amba's eyes gleamed with sudden fire as she spotted the familiar face. It was Nathan Ray!

"No! It's Nathan! I know him. Wait, don't shoot!"

"Can you trust him?"

"Wait…he is with…That is Rodh!"

The vehicle came to a standstill only a few feet away with a tremendous jolt. The urgency of their situation was such that Amba and Nakul needed no invitation, and the very next moment, they were speeding away in the van. Nathan quickly apprised Amba of the events which occurred after she escaped; how he managed to escape the prison with the help of an old guard, a *Habishi*, in exchange for a transfer to another prison; apparently, the guard had had enough of the mad Colonel's perversities.

Rodh's words poured as deadly poison in her ears.

"Many of our people were killed by the Red-Hounds. It was a massacre. They forcibly took every able-bodied man and woman, boy and girl, with them. Only the oldies and the disabled have been left behind to rot with no food and their shelters destroyed. Those who were wounded and they couldn't take, they killed. Why, even the cows and the hens and the goats were not spared!"

"There is nothing that Madbull is not capable of," Nathan added. "No barbarity which he won't commit, if only to get back. He held me captive after you got away from the prison so he could remain safe. Which is why, my escape maddened him beyond words. He has gone crazy; been picking up the youths, the ones somehow left alive, from your village. His men also attacked the caves where Tanu Bakar and his men were hiding. The ones not dead have been taken…except Tanu Bakar—!"

Nathan stopped talking when he noticed Amba's expression change suddenly. It was her turn to reveal that it was too late now for Tanu Bakar. A shocked Rodh descended into a mournful silence at her words.

"There is no time to mourn. We have to hurry and find a place to hide before night falls," said Nathan to Rodh, before turning to Amba. "You're lucky you're alive! We were afraid we would be too late. But the goddess of Hori truly watches over you."

Or the witch, Amba said to herself, touching her amulet.

23

Fear is not like fury. It comes in stages that cannot be numbered and pinned like beetles in boxes. One cannot taxonomise or make it sensible. Amba felt her world overflow with great fear for her people. Nausea mingled with the terrible possibilities that obtruded into her imagination; she felt maddened, and also fearful, that, in the midst of a catastrophe, she would not be able to stop the worst from happening.

"When I was at Baikaal, I heard some guards talk about heavy offloading of fuel cans into trucks, along with explosives and weapons. Men boasting about some *definite solution* they had in mind for the *Habishis*."

"Definite solution?"

"What about Tara? Did they take her, too?" Nakul asked in panic.

"No. They probably thought a pregnant woman could do them no harm. But they did kill her cow." Amba exchanged a look with Nakul. His body sagged as he stared back wildly at her.

The wrongness of even discussing this was indescribable to her. What hellish vengeance did Madbull plan to execute? And to what extent was he prepared to go? Amba's demeanour seemed to grow cold as the initial feeling of bewilderment turned to confusion. Soon, every inch of her skin crawled with rising rage. She was shaking and unable to hold still.

"Maybe he took them all to Baikaal prison?" asked Amba.

"I don't think he ever intended to take them to the prison," Nathan's reply chilled her to the bone, each word a loaded gun. "There is every possibility he plans to wipe out the evidence of his deed, stage some accident, blame the whole thing on the villagers. Eliminate the evidence completely."

"They are criminals, Amba. Unscrupulous, ruthless men with no morals. The men he has chosen are not official Regiment—they are the Red-Hounds, chosen specially for their ability to commit unimaginable atrocities."

No one spoke for the rest of the journey. Nathan sat apart, insular and incommunicable. Nakul seemed tranquil and sad. It was a lonely journey, hard and dreary, with no one talking to the other, perhaps urged by a dread of the unknown.

When something jammed the vehicle's wheels, no one thought it was serious. But the cloudburst soon turned the road into a mini river, and the way the trees swayed, they could be crushed as a bug in a glass cup. Dropping the gears into low range, the van moved a couple of notches into the emergency brakes and allowed the engine to pull them, but they were stuck in a crater and the engine stopped. Nathan slammed on the accelerator, which was a wrong move, as the vehicle went ahead a few metres before it started sinking into the rising slush. The engine refused to shudder to life. The vehicle was stuck in ten feet of mire and inching dangerously towards a black-brownish open gorge of gushing water. It hit a bump as it came out, with a massive heave, and her head banged on the metallic rim of the door several times with tremendous force.

Amba, who was seated in the back, tried to stand up. The vehicle's door suddenly gave outwards. Caught unawares, she started slipping but Nakul, sitting across her, reacted instinctively and pulled her to safety and firmly closed the door. Bog-covered craters became common as they journeyed, sometimes single, sometimes in cluster, and they picked their way carefully past the julienned remnants of unrooted cajeput trees flung on all sides. The passengers sat in hushed silence, hypnotised by the rapid turn of events. The sky was rusty water and the trees blurred to ink. Electric scent of the storm carried in with the rising wind. Amba lay flat on her back in the vehicle as images passed by, till it was an unending procession, a continuum of ochre and green.

They were expecting it, but it still came as a shock when the hill lit up with lights; erupted in whizzing, flashing, banging. Crimson starbursts covered the sky above their heads. The first big explosive kicked off from the barge with an impressive noise. The artillery cracked into the air, throwing sparks, and everyone ducked for cover.

Amba felt the concussive thump in her chest and heard the crack of the report in a tight sequence. When it hit, they felt the kick, the overpressure came in and, the next instant, the vehicle was lit with steel fragments all over the compartment. It was a miracle the fuel tank remained clear. Another rocket exploded behind them, lighting up an arc and throwing light on a battered, concrete divider, some fifty metres away. Nathan tumbled into her and she fell back when the tires of the vehicle squealed to avoid the blast and the doors spun to the right and a blaze of fire shone through the door. The force of the explosion catapulted Nakul and Rodh onto each other, the last thing she saw for several moments, as the flash of light through the open door blinded her. She pushed back to try to balance herself when the familiar hiss of the rockets was followed by more explosions.

Bullets whizzed overhead, and this time, she recognised the distinct bark of the modernised combat weapon. She grabbed a firearm, extended it across the seat, turned her head, and fired a round through the window. She lost count of the shots, which missed her by inches and her heart hammered in her chest. The vehicle swerved and dived and sank into unseen depressions, just recklessly enough and not a fraction more, its nose to the ground, now up in the air, whining as frantically as it rushed, to avoid being hit, leaping abruptly at right angles, braking sharply to avoid the void.

A shot hit its mark and the vehicle's fuel tank blew up. The fireball illuminated a vast stretch of the field, and when she turned her face away from the bonfire. The vehicle halted its gyrations at such an angle that, for some time, the windows did not look into the road but the sky. It was an even more frightening descent as the vehicle fell back to the earth like shattered fragments of a clay pigeon. It all happened in bare few seconds. The next instant, she was in a smouldering slag heap of exuding pungent stink of burning fuel. Nathan was stretched flat on the ground, choking and coughing. A hand squeezed hers and she realised she was still alive. No one saw it. They were focusing on the sky, the forest, the river.

Braaaaaaaaakkkkkkkkkkkkkk!!!

The piercing sound suspended all thinking. It was the groan chasing the clap. The shockwave knocked her on her back and bits of dirt and gravel rained down on her face. Another grenade went off, its giant claws tearing the skies apart, leaving everyone deaf and nauseous.

The first thing which came to mind was that she did not want to die by fire. She knew what fire did to the human body;

she had seen enough carbonised corpses fused into metal, with teeth exposed in a permanent simian rictus, the flesh of the lips and faces melted off, no longer recognisable as anything which was ever alive. Amba feared nothing more than ending in fire.

It was blazing hot and heat poured up from the ground she could hardly open her eyes. Drops of sweat rolled onto her lips, tasting of salt and dust. She bit her lip and licked all around, just to get more of it. Anything to clear the smell of fuel and sulphur out of her mouth.

A sickening realisation slowly dawned on her.

Nakul was not with her anymore. Amba turned onto her stomach to look for him. She made it to her knees and, disoriented, searched for her gun confusedly. Her eyes focused on a familiar shape ahead. It rolled over clumsily on the road; its limbs bent at odd angles.

She clenched her teeth and kept going, though she could hardly feel her legs. Or the rest of her body. And could barely walk. She took a step towards the shape at the centre of the road ahead. Her hearing came back with a gush and she heard shouting and more shots. Amba regained her balance and took another step, feeling returned to her hands and feet. She made it about twenty metres, before another device went off. It came from her left side in a sickly grey puff. Fragments clipped her leg and she lost her balance and cartwheeled over. Her left cheek hit the ground before the rest of her.

"Stay down! Stay down! They are firing again!"

"I am going to Nakul."

"No, Amba."

"But we have to go to him. Can you not see him? There he is," she said slowly, as if explaining to a dimwit.

"You cannot help him now," Nathan said, as gently as he could.

"I saw him roll over. I can get to him," she said, wholly unheeding her own injuries.

Nathan moved closer to her. He held her arms to stop her from moving. She threw an elbow at his ribs. Tried to break the grip. She thrashed hard and managed to break free for a second, until he wrapped his elbow under her shoulder, put his palm on the back of her neck and forced her right onto the ground.

Her cheek scraped against the black asphalt, hot as hell.

"Please, let me go. Nathan. Let me go and get my brother."

"Nakul is dead. He died, Amba."

No, no, no, no, no!

She thrashed violently at the words, though, in reality, she hardly got her hips off the ground. Nathan had her pinned with her arms out in the front, palms flat out. Clarity returned and she could just see the shape of Nakul. She dug her nails into the pavement and burnt her fingertips, as if trying to dig her way to him. The shooting stopped again, but the silence was deceptive.

"Fuck you! Let me go!"

"Listen—look to your right," Nathan whispered. There was something in his tone which made her stop. She turned to look. She knew what it was the moment she set her eyes on it. A black curbstone which was not set in concrete like the others. It was a different black, too. More grey, and it looked new. No scuff marks. Buried rounds were daisy-chained with detonation cord. They were trapped at the centre of the kill zone.

The click-clack of weapons had slowed down. A final shower of artillery shells revealed the apocalyptic scene below. The growing din swelled to a tremendous chorus, accompanied by blurred forms of troops who filled the field. They were hemmed in by the men, swarthy and wild-looking, wearing belts and red shirts. They fell into their places at the sides, in front and in the rear; a fully concentrated force surrounded them whole.

"To the slaughter with you—*witch*!" they chanted. Rough hands seized her and dragged her by the hair. She stopped resisting and lay her head on the ground, limp. For as long as she could, she kept staring at Nakul's still shape on the road and the dark sheen around it. It was the last time she would see him. She was stunned by the intensity of the grief she felt; a bitter paradox, that she ended up losing Nakul just when she had found him.

24

A kind of sky under which nothing good happens. The sun stuck, in all its malevolence, to a fleshy vastness that stretched endlessly like the residue of a nightmare. The captives, tied roughly with ropes around their necks and hands, forced to walk all the way down the broken stony path that led to the clearing below. An unforgiving quarter-mile trudge before they reached their destination, exhausted and demoralised.

Nothing could prepare them for the sight that greeted them. Villagers—men and women—had been forcibly enclosed behind barbed wires, lined up, without pretence, next to the propane tanks, which reclined like rows of sleeping demons, their swollen, white bellies glinting in the sun, promising grim redemption. They looked bad and smelled worse; sun-roasted bony faces, bleached lips and mangy hair, dehydrated frames enclosed in crusty, chapped skin. Waiting for its slaughter, this mess of humanity was a new kind of species.

But the real horror stood a few metres away. Forced inside a large box-like cage, the younger men were packed cheek to jowl to keep them under control. The packed interiors of the box, lit with the ghostly blue backout light looked like the alimentary canal of a whale. Some men squatted on the floor; the thinner ones perched on their knees; the contours of skin, separating one individual from another, merged; and everyone was forced into mandatory intimacy, which made them look less human. The heat in the close confine soon climbed up over forty degrees Celsius; so did the intensity of the odour—the stink of sweat, of unwashed clothes, of fake perfume, cheap leather, plastic purses, and of anxiety; the only succour being the breeze through the openings, guarded by Red-Hounds carrying firearms with a twenty-round magazine.

The guards passed their time teasing the caged men, while a few even gave vent to their bloodlust and malignant hate by menacing gestures, sending their families into an apoplexy of fear. Fathers wept for their families, living and those lost, and mothers trembled for the fate of their children.

Her face blanched at the piteous state of her brethren, her people, her uncles and aunts and neighbours and their children their families. A slaughter awaited. A bloody mess of a slaughter. There was no question. They would be slaughtered. Every one of them.

Madbull finally made an appearance, wearing a large hat and a massive jacket which greatly enhanced his height and the wideness of his shoulders. Wickedness emanated from him in waves. His huge jaws seemed to drip with a reddish flame and the small, deep-set, cruel eyes were ringed with fire as he addressed the gathering. There was murder in the cowardly hearts of his men, and stupidity and lust and cruelty and greed, most of all. His snarl incorporated all that was vicious, malignant when his gaze fell on Nathan Ray.

"What an annoying man you are, Nathan Ray! Here I was imagining all things horrible, going out of my mind thinking about the sanctions you will get the government to impose on me. You should have run while you had the chance. Look at you, now. I hear these witches have a way of getting under a man's skin!"

"Stop this madness while there is still time, Madbull."

"You are in no position to command me, dear Nathan Ray. You have chosen your side, that with the *Habishi* girl—this false witch. You could not live by my rules, now you all will die by them. The false witch and the false saviour!" Madbull turned to his men and said, "These barbarians have endangered our lives, our families, our businesses—No more! The vermin should be exterminated."

"Madbull, if you think your crimes won't be discovered, you are wrong—!"

"These people you see in front of you are not humans like us, Nathan. They are wild animals in human skin who pray to witches. Why should they die civilised deaths?"

Wails of horror erupted at his words. Women beat their chests and the men looked fearful of the fate that awaited them and their families. Some threw themselves on the soldiers' feet, only to be kicked back with sticks and rifle butts.

"Civilisation will enter the Hori valley and the witch-worshipping barbarians will be thrown out. An end to the terror of the damned false witches!" Rosie Madbull roared.

An answering growl went up. Clenched fists were raised.

"The old witch too died a very painful death, as she well deserved," he said with conscious cruelty and with a sense of delight born out of that cruelty. Goaded by his words, the mood of the gathering became much more aggressive. Combative. Explosive. The growl of the blood-hungry crowd was fever pitch as Madbull displayed Patala's chopped fingers. There were quite a few of his men who clapped and begged for a memento to take home. The features of the captors were not discernible, for there was a grotesqueness about them which was alike.

"I promise you all a grand event—a spectacle you will never forget. Blown from a gun—that's how the false witch's throat will be torn out of her, so she doesn't curse, and her eyes will be gouged out, so she doesn't see, and her heart will be burned, so she never breathes again!"

The killing procedure was described with relish. The upper part of the small of Amba's back, Madbull explained with gusto, would be rested against the muzzle of the old cannon gun. When the gun would be fired, her head would go straight up into the air, some forty or fifty feet. Her arms would fly off right and left, high up in the air, and fall at, perhaps, a hundred-yard distance. And the legs would drop to the ground beneath the muzzle of the gun.

Inside the cage, the air was thick with the smell of fear.

The front rank of the policemen cocked their guns, obviously responding to an order, and a chill of anxiety ran through. A wave of panic spread from one person to another, anguished voices of men straining against the cage. A fresh disturbance in the dense front part of the crowd broke out, accompanied with protesting shouts.

Sudden cries ripped Amba back to the sight of unarmed civilian masses pressing themselves onto walls with nowhere to run; but the Red-Hounds were too wild, too quick for them. Rodh snatched a gun from a guard and brandished his weapon, daring anyone to come close to him.

"Come on, now, hand over the gun," said Madbull in a placatory tone, which sounded awkward, coming from a man for whom cruelty sprung fast as weed.

Rodh fired a warning shot and that drew a line. He was joined by several young men who had managed to amass stones and rocks to use as missiles. Then, one of the youth stepped out of the ranks and did something unimaginable. He knocked off Madbull's hat and shoved him to the ground like flotsam in the wild, raging torrent.

Like a hunting dog calling its quarry, Madbull's voice echoed off the mountain, raw and baying, and the guns went live. The unmistakable sound of metal going through flesh. A meaty thumping. A housewife beating a dusty carpet. The wild panic led people to stampede in order to run from the death raining from guns. Several men tried to run towards the exit, but the panic-struck villagers also had the same idea and they ended up stumbling and tripping upon each other. Those who managed to get out, kept their whimpering heads below, and when something whizzed overhead, shrapnel or a bullet, some fell to the earth and began crawling.

The headman's daughter's child got hit by a bullet and it died instantaneously. Crazed with grief, she rushed towards Madbull in fury. He pushed her back with such a force that the child's corpse got flung from her arms. She rushed to pick her child up when Madbull's bullets hit her. She got thrown back abruptly, as though she reached the end of an invisible leash. She stayed on her feet for a few seconds, even after the bullets came out of her back at the level of her breasts. The two entry wounds in her chest like dark, red roses on the white cloth, she collapsed on her knees, her eyes wide open. Rodh's head was split and blood flowed freely down his face. Another youth lost his footing and sprawled forwards on his stomach. Immediately, a hundred legs trampled him. The scent of freshly spilled blood worked the crowd into a delirium.

Still on his feet, Rodh was driven against the wall, a medal torn from his jacket. There was a fleck of blood on his mouth where an elbow struck him and he struggled with the flap of the holster on his belt. He was too late. The Red-Hounds were too densely packed around him to aim properly. He fired blindly from the hip. The shot made a huge noise and a man screamed in pain and shock and the crowd backed away as the man fell down on the floor, clutching his stomach. Rodh was now surrounded by the animal growl of the crowd closing in on him. He tried to pull back but the crowd barred his exit. Angry faces, swollen with hate, mouthed abuses and fisted his face.

Madbull's orders came like quick lashes of the whip.

Snap. Swish. Snap.

The bayonet cut an arc in the sky and hit Rodh on his face and dragged down to his chest. There was a bright flash of blood, which dripped in a thin line from below his eye. Four men caught him and threw him on the ground and one of them straddled his stomach, pinning Rodh under him. With a single stroke, the blade cut through his shirt and split his belly open from neck to groin. Madbull looked satisfied, almost wildly elated, with the butchery even as Rodh lay dying, writhing in pain.

The air was rent by the shrieks and lamentations of the women, who were casting off their ornaments and tearing their hair. The cries sounded like the last sound that a million victims have ever heard, the sound heard by thousands from nameless tribes who perished in innumerable, forgotten killing grounds of the defeated.

When Amba finally managed to pulled her eyes away from the carnage, her expression was horrified. Even Nathan, who had witnessed shootings and slaughters earlier, had never seen anything like that before, and felt damned for it.

But no battle is decided in a single moment. In every battle, there arise moments of unexpected and fortuitous intervention, on which the results depend. One such intervention was about to take place in this battle, too, which would decisively turn its outcome. Madbull, in his supreme arrogance, did not expect anything. The sequence of events about to unfold was about to take him by complete surprise; one, which would rapidly culminate into unbridged horror.

It started with the sudden drop in temperature.

Then, it went strangely quiet. An undecipherable, naturalistic morse code occupied the air, and the only thing which seemed certain was that what one could not fully comprehend or stop or reverse, had been set into motion.

An icy dew chilled the faces of those present. Announcing the coming of some new terror. No one could remember the air ever seeming that high or that cold and rarefied; a moment, which would mark the turning. Men tucked in closer, with the women and the children in the centre. The Red-Hounds, already jumpy, loaded their guns and lifted them into high port positions and started brandishing and firing towards the forest. Their baffled gaze went to where the trees hunched over oddly, conspiring predators. A faint susurration, a humming vibration metastasised from across the forest.

"The devil is here— "

"They are coming, they are coming!"

"Monsters!"

"The witch's curse! Oh god, save us—"

"Fools, stop your gibbering!" shouted Madbull, but despite their new guns and stocked-up ammo and shining artillery, the Red-Hounds looked nervous. The knowledge of being watched by a hundred eyes, not entirely of this world, overwhelmed them.

At first, only leaves and twigs and small stones got sucked in. Then, larger stones and rocks started flying and shrubs were uprooted. Violent eddies of wind gust dirt and leaf into mini tornados, and the soil cracked, exposing old graves, long overgrown with weeds. Several green sparks swirled in the air, silent fireworks going down a plug hole. Instead of vanishing, when they reached the centre of the vortex, they clumped together until they formed an amorphous blob the size of an average man.

"Don't be fooled. These appearances, which bewilder you, are merely electrical phenomena, not uncommon—it will stop!" shouted Madbull, and just as suddenly it had begun, it stopped.

"See? Did I not say there is nothing magical? There is no witchery at play here."

"We should finish the job and get out of here."

"Look, look! Oh god! Look!"

"They are here—they are here!"

"All around, they are all around— I can feel their eyes, their teeth—"

"Mercy, god!"

The still air gusted in a twister and created a miasma, which began to spin round and round on an entirely different axis; and the axis changed every second.

Around the malevolent miasma, a base stench was gaining. Of whatever sordid sicknesses a feeble sun could summon. The stench had lingered over hundreds of years, of cowardice and greed. Time and again, they were banished into vessels, where they waited, biding their time, feeding, gathering strength.

Gripped by a feeling of being in the presence of shadows, much larger much more powerful than them, the men got more fearful and, feeding on the men's fear, the presence seemed to get stronger and stronger. The 'smog' shrank, became denser. It seemed to form into a foetus of sorts—a bulge for a head and four buds coming from a curved spine. The 'entity' was maturing and spreading its milky whiteness; a thick mist gone crazy, it moved without constraint in any direction. The miasma spun round and settled on them for a brief moment, blocking out the view for a few hundred yards. When it dissipated, the warehouse was empty. There was not a soul in sight.

"Gone, gone! They are all gone! The men in the cage…the villagers!"

One of the men gibbered stupidly, pointing at the empty space. The families kneeling on the ground a moment ago, too, were gone.

Each one of them—*vanished into thin air!*

"W-what devilry is this?!"

"But how is it possible? They were here a moment ago!"

"The devil is here! We are doomed!"

"It's the witch doing her sorcery!"

"Look, look—there it is!"

"God, save us!"

"What the—"

"I saw her lips moving! She is casting a curse on us!"

"Burn her! Burn her!"

"Be quiet! I will put an end to her sorcery, then, first! I will gouge out her tongue so she cannot cast her curse. I will not take out her eyes, yet I want her to see her people burn before her eyes!" Madbull said in false bravado.

"No…Burn the witch! Take out her eyes! Look at her lips, they are moving!"

"She is cursing us!"

"Summoning the devil—that is what she is doing! Kill her, kill her!"

Amba had a strange sensation, as if her consciousness had, at a certain point of time, forked off into two branches. Words came from her mouth—words she did not recognise—even as another voice, which she knew was her own, pleaded for sanity.

Something shifted in her head.

Something huge.

Then, everything she saw collapsed into something else.

She blinked.

It looked the same.

It wasn't.

It seemed she could not see them at all.

That she had slipped entirely out of their world and moved into another, wilder world, from which humans had been completely erased.

She choked, almost scared of waking up what was half-asleep inside her and snorting out powdery-thin shrieks with each breathe. She imagined she was standing on the back of a creature's brackish orange tissue, waiting for the executioner to awake.

The rage which came upon her was vast. And it came out of nowhere and everywhere. It was the rage of something not fitting and she was the thing that did not fit and she was the one smashing it over and over again with bloodied hands. The air around her bristled and she seemed convulsed with a fierce, unreasoning rage. Soon, blind-cold, shaking fury rose and rose and rose, till all the rage, which crouched inside her, was free.

Something was changing in her. She shivered. It was as if the air was contracting to a point. Unseen needs were motoring through her and she was ravenous.

In a strange language, she summoned the entities inside her.

But they never came alone—

To participate in the ceremony of ordeals—

They dragged other things along.

⌘ CEREMONY OF ORDEALS ⌘

We had no choice but to come when She summoned Us.

But We never come alone. We drag Others along. To participate in the ceremony of ordeals.

We were the hunters now—Our mind of a hard, unyielding nature. And the predominant idea of revenge had taken such complete possession that there was no room for any other emotion.

She summoned Us to unleash the truth of Her. There was no ambiguity in the command. And We were more than ready. And hungry.

But the truth of Her was overwhelming, an immensity, which even We would struggle to fully comprehend.

25

The world erupted in a primeval chaos. Noxious sulphur surge of unbridled hate and fury invaded her lungs as she transformed into a weapon unleashed. The Furies inside her worked up her rage into that of a driven beast.

She did not strive to control them but allowed herself to be borne away by the stream of unabated torments, and soon she would bend her mind towards inflicting maximum injury and horrible death. Images of Nakul and Tanu Bakar and Patala and the slaughtered bodies of the villagers and the fresh horror of Rodh's gruesome end filled her with such an intense hate that she could not breathe.

How else, unless she hated with all her being, could she destroy them?

She knew that the hunting would take her to the very edge of being a human. Then, it would take her past that place to something which was not human at all.

Amba willed her old self out of her mind; the world seemed to close off in darkness. Suddenly, within the space of minutes, she achieved what she didn't even know she had internally wished for; justified herself to herself, and without lie or subterfuge, without fear or shame, she cut the cord forever, with her former self.

However, she experienced no loss of awareness, for new parts of her consciousness filled her, the ones she was unaware of—the ones she had ignored.

She felt inexhaustible, incapable of fatigue. Face aglow with an otherworldly shine, she stood calmly smiling, a huntress of a corralled game.

She was one with that which was inside her. She was whole.

Fully contaminated.

Fully pure.

Her body seemed to split into millions of fragments, each retaining her whole consciousness, dragged into different directions by abnormal forces. Her flesh felt shredded, her joints torn apart, her bones smashed, but she felt infinitely more sharpened by the changes happening to her.

Inside her, a terrifying alchemy was at play. It seemed the earth under her had ripped into half and she was swallowed and vomited out and every sound grew loud and louder and her ears bled, blood and skin turned inside out.

Her skin flared white.

White as the fire's heart, purest as the hottest coals.

And then, the heat came rolling over all with a sound of roaring waves, blistering skin, crushing breath from chests. There was no air. She had taken it all.

The transformation of Amba was amazing, stupefying.

In the sweep of natural savagery, she who was at once also human, but also ceased to be so, but still could, at any moment, become a woman again.

Knees of men strong in battle trembled when they saw it—Her.

Darting in and out of the white fog, open-mouthed, she came. Jaws foaming, roaring with fury, she lashed her tail from side to side, about her ribs and loins, and glared as she sprang. Too late to save but not too late to avenge.

No one could think of pitting their puny strength against the iron muscles and brutal ferocity of this enraged beast of an unknown world; in fact, the only outcome of such an encounter would be painful death.

She presided over the assembly of visions, as they did her bidding; she was calm and detached. A noise of an invisible boulder drawn across the earth and suddenly, grey blurs tumbled past and the sucking sound of the whirlpool reached across, an assembly of phantasms. A procession of one feral beast after another. Their faces were slightly elongated. Sickly scale flecked green, eyes crimson. A blood-hungry roar like nothing he had heard before. Like wild animals letting loose more of their roars, faces disfigured, discoloured, the reptilian half-breeds, they were demons tearing into the Regiment.

Nathan felt sick but he couldn't look away.

It couldn't be. Couldn't.

Gaping in frozen horror at what lay underneath her!

The apparition which confronted them first, the thing so like Amba, yet so unlike her.

A thing unexpected and undreamed with eyes, burning with the power of a stare into the unknown. Then its face shrivelled, which was no face at all, had a thin, fantastic haze, as it were, with traces of human likeness, shifting to and fro, across its countenance, sometimes vanishing entirely, but growing more perceptible than ever with the next whiff of wind. A soulless, pitiless being, not human, but one who lost their humanity in some transformation.

The next one was huge. It was white and grey burned onto the depths. Pumped up with its poisonous vapours, the miasma exhaled. It gained in tenor and frequency, all monstrosities, each and every blinding one, existed everywhere and nowhere all at once, and there was not a soul which did not pale in front of the expanding and contracting hysteria of the ghastly immensity before them.

Slowly it came into focus—an object looked at through a telescope, except this phantom was close. Very close. And moved with an eerie rasping voice, moaning, groaning. The miasma uncoiled itself and aggressively pressed forward till it filled the entire path from side to side and end to end.

Now they could see the form of a woman, with a silvery ragged line across her neck, where she was hung, and gaunt, soulless eyes.

This new apparition was burnt, no hair, no eyebrows, features melted and raw. Her form twisted in ghastly contortions, arms, heads, legs bent in incredible ways, as those who fall from great heights, dumped from the sky itself, finally recognisable as Patala.

Patala smiled a ghost of a smile.

From the dream, from the night of shrouded terrors, from maggots and worms, she seemed to uncurl and stretch herself. Her eyes closed in on the soldiers, oblivious in their sweating fear. She crept closer. A reptilian stench wafted about her. Most of her body was still not visible. She looked grey as the air, as the mist that covered Hori itself. When she screamed, the sound was piercing chaos—the sound of a hundred wolves howling at once. Some of the soldiers dropped their guns to cover their ears.

She was not alone.

The wind shot and chattered back and there was a whirling sound in the sky, a whistle which rose and dropped and circled and moaned and shoals of birds exploded around rocks.

Patala's mother stared about her, eyes dead holes in grey flesh. The miasma screamed again. Its breath washed over her stink and scorching heat. Craving the taste of mortal flesh, the body sagged out of the mist. Gelatinous and huge.

It made a terrifying noise and the men discovered scorching fear. As they neared her, she tore out as twisting shadows wielding death—pierced the soldier's breast, skewered them like meat, ripped open their spine, and blood spattered as their insides spilled out. Burning blinding rage. Its neck began to ripple and bunch back on itself. She was gathering to strike. The soldiers could see the stains of old blood around her mouth, the shreds of flesh still hanging from her teeth. Splinters flew, men went tumbling about.

A gust of wind. A shifting of foliage. A buzz of angry bees. From the dark, they poured out a new batch of horrors. A mad chatter of disembodied mob of beasts. Building rank upon rank, from all sides, they spilled to the sides of the perimeter until they completely surrounded the encampment, hemming in the structure, which now resembled a cluster of rectangular islands in a noisy restless sea.

Each creature stood around seven-to-ten-feet high at the shoulder and up to two-and-a-half feet from head to tail and looked no less than a hundred kilos in weight. A column of creatures in different shapes and sizes. Beard flipping in the air, dribbling from their mouths.

The Red-Hounds fired indiscriminately and the toughest men formed a circle of defence around Madbull and a vehicle moved towards the centre to evacuate the Colonel. The column of beasts came to a halt and the growling stopped. At a signal, the formation resumed rapidly, with two creatures standing back to back, and other such sets standing at a distance of three hands, drawing up seven circles, keeping an eye on their main target.

With the combination of the olive-green fur and the brown stripes across the back, they were virtually invisible among the bush and tall grasses their prey fed upon. They moved in a pattern around them, shifting continuously, impossible to pin. The beasts pounced on and engaged briefly with the Red-Hounds and advanced. Their place was taken up by the next rank of beasts on either side, who again engaged the opponent briefly and then advanced in a circular pattern towards the centre. The last of the pack gave a signal of having completed the formation and the pack members, who, so far had been facing outwards, turn inwards to face the opponent. The oblivious enemy realised too late that it was surrounded on all sides by seven tiers of beasts.

A hot wind blew from their bloodied mouths and the ground shook from the impact of their heavy hooves as they leapt towards Madbull.

The Colonel was hit by pure fear, bright as the sun.

It dug claws into his eyes. Bit into his bones. Ripped tissues. Mauled limbs. A hundred claws and teeth.

A crazed Madbull fired at the beasts and men alike. Many of his own men fell to his bullets. The balloon rose as it expanded; the howls of the brutal horde, in the delirium of their orgy, made a tight circle around him. But, at length, it borne away towards the south, with Madbull in tow.

Rosie Madbull had completely vanished. As if he had never been. It was going to be the last anyone ever saw of Colonel Rosie Madbull.

They were gone, too, the complexities, the phantasms, the miasma—all of it. All that remained were carbonised tree trunks and charcoaled branches in the steaming, fetid air.

When the sticky dust settled, the little dark heaps that lay on the ground outside were slowly revealed as men, and their guns lay abandoned in the aftermath of the bloodbath. Soldiers lay strewn across, limbs and heads at awkward angles, entrails bursting out of stomachs. The belated storm arrived born on black winds, as if an afterthought, striking with a flat hand of mindless fury, wiped off the blood from where the bodies of the dead lay.

Amba looked about at the deaths with sorrow. It was not a patronising sorrow; it was the sorrow of all deaths. She was accountable for those deaths. For the first time in her life, she had been a perpetrator. But she also realised she was accountable to herself, to this world and to all the things in it, as much as the other world.

It happened when Amba was emerging in her original form. A rifle had cracked to her right, and though she did not hear the bullet in passing, the thud of it came to her ears when it struck a palm trunk farther on.

She felt something was very wrong when, without uttering any potent words and without any peculiar gesture, she found herself knocked on the ground with great force. This was followed by a flash of crimson and a burning pain at the core of her diaphragm. She registered, with surprise, the rapid spread of red on her chest, wondering, did a bullet do that? Stray bullets had found several marks on her body. Amba felt dizzy and heavy and sick from the loss of so much blood. She watched from a distance above, her futile attempts to prevent the blood from gushing out by cupping the wound with the ham-handed fists of a child and realised, with soft wonder, the times she had seen this happening, the dreams which had been prophecies.

As she lay there, her life slipping out, she realised she had always believed in the *witches*. But ever since she could remember, she had always hated the word. Perhaps because she had hated the customs and the people who intervened between her and *them*. And it was a sudden discovery like finding ground under your feet, or an unexpected awareness. This was the *witch* she had found through sacrificing her life, through her flesh being cut, her nails being torn, her skin being ripped, her blood sucked away.

Her witch had no form, no doctrine, no scriptures, no rules, no morals, no logic, no reward, no punishment. Only magic, for its own sake, weaving and unwoven. It did not take away and there was no heaven in the sky, no hell down below for it.

The rear light of consciousness began to fade into a distance, sucked into the depths of the night—and all that remained was the sound of the wind slipping through, and Amba felt herself dwindling, utterly dispersed to the elements, randomised like vapours released from a balloon.

Nathan found Amba with gore drying stiff upon her stone-cold cheeks. Her arms were greasy with the death vapours as she lay still near the waters. The bullets had caught her on her chest and stomach and the impact lifted her from the cordite-covered black soil and flung her across into the moss-covered embankment.

He felt for her heartbeat with his bare fingers and shivered and drew his hand back. Superstitious, perhaps, to think that any flickering sign of life she showed, his attention might somehow stop it. She smelled of pepper and musk and burned stone and melting metal. There was a strange silvery tint to her that is felt, rather than seen; a kind of silvery light, like a rainy sky reflected from the surface of a river, remote from thought or emotion as a patch of sky. Like the world, and those not of the world too could not touch her anymore.

One moment, she seemed a creature shaped by millions of years of evolution for a life she had not yet lived, the next her eyes were luminous and her mouth half-open in the final death sigh.

⌘ THE COMING ⌘

Every time We hunted, She took part wholeheartedly, becoming the extension of Us, but every time We committed a killing, She pulled Herself back from Us into being a human again.

Hunting made Her connect to Us. But the regret and the grief She felt from the death of a prey distinguished Her from Us. It made Her human. And that was the difference between Her and Us. That was the great puzzle. And it was destined to be played out again and again.

We could never be a singular entity. She was too independent. The borders between Her and Us lay somewhere between Our hunt and Her grief.

Thoughts light as ether, and then so dense, no mind could contain them; thoughts rolling and spinning over and over, as She went down the current, right to the stage when it all began. When all Her future was seeded. In the stage after that, everything registered as incomprehensible chaos.

The awakening was mind-numbingly painful. Giving birth to one's own body would have inflicted lesser pain. Each nerve cell, detached from its skin, pulsating back to life; each cell, filling again with living blood, the muscle snapping back in shape, Her shattering screams would have been heard at the bottom of the valley. There were time lapses. Dangerous cracks through which the vessel could slip.

Living in multiple realities, floating loosely between them, forgetting what each one was as soon as She moved into a new one. She could be trapped between realms.

She tried to force Her way back, tried to wake up several times. The gates to Her human world kept getting shut before She could come over.

When She stopped breathing, Her soul crumbled into cold smoke. It felt neither hungry nor thirsty; no warmth, a formless gruel. She reached the outer extremities of existence. She was minimal. Tissues and bones held Her in and kept the world out. Her soul, released from the cage of flesh, sped out to the extremities, curl across its surface, frothing like waves, causing dreams to come like bubbles of burrowing clams. There was no before, no after; She moved and stayed still; it had happened and was happening; there remained a core within and, in the core, a pulse, and on the skin, a sense of opposing and concurrent wills.

When She was barely physical, We came closer to the surface several times. She offered no resistance. She was in no position to offer any. We interfered with time, struggled to turn it backwards, to when life was perhaps leaving from the blank walls, to discover an opening or speck of light—and We found it.

We seeded. And grew and grew and grew, till We enveloped the whole of Her. Plugged all the holes. At a point, She stopped leaking out.

26

On its ancient watery bed bloated with bleached bones, the Iravati continued its smooth and timeless tread down the Hori mountains. Flowing endlessly, never sleeping, lined by thousands of years old rocks, carved deep by rain and wind, by the claws of countless scrabbling lizards, by the seeds which got stuck and sprouted from their cracks. It rolled past the evacuated villages, full of lost dreams, past the empty compounds, blackened fields, past the soils once drenched red with blood. Waters always wipe it all clean, wash out all traces, erase the very air, as if nothing happened. The telling remains will gently sink down the abyss, lost forever.

Nathan Ray knew he was not mad. The inexplicability of what he witnessed on that night of horrors months ago did not mean that he succumbed to some form of mass psychosis, along with the terrified villagers. But what he had witnessed was not delirium, it was as obvious as the taste of blood in his mouth.

It happened.

It existed.

It exists. Quiet and dangerous. It was everywhere in the air, under the earth, in the leaves, the waters, in the flowers and the seeds. His mind struggled to build across the gap, to make a new inhabitable world of sense.

As for the events of that fateful night, no one would ever agree on conclusively. The *Habishi* villagers were superstitious and went into a consensual silence; but even when a few gathered the wits and courage, their fantastical versions, at best, could be put down to unverified gibber. Astonished state officials inquiring the matter concluded 'self-hypnosis', while others suggested 'spiritism based on tribal superstitions'. It was assumed that the apparitions conjured were nothing more than a super mass hallucination, induced by excitement and fear. Though the peculiar markings near the site of the incident, where Madbull was last seen, and on the bodies of the dead men, remain unexplained.

"Strange," the judge muttered, "strange and most strange."

He left it at that.

A Jail Committee, headed by a new Magistrate, was appointed to look into the illegal acts committed by Colonel Rosie Madbull and the remaining members of Madbull's Red-Hound army were transported where they belonged—permanently locked inside Baikaal. The new jailor noted with surprise that the prisoners seemed relieved to be secure behind the prison walls from 'whatever is out there'. Colonel Rosie Madbull's crimes were judged 'criminally reprehensible' and the state expressed that it was obliged to exert the full force of the law to bring the 'perpetrator to justice'. Several search teams were dispatched to look for the missing Colonel. However, despite all efforts, Madbull was never traced—dead or alive.

The whole affair turned out to be advantageous, in part, for the state, as most of the villagers agreed to leave the *Habishis'* land in exchange for a tidy sum of money and relocate to the plains. As the news spread in the media, the state came in for criticism for exploiting the villagers who, according to the reporter, "were being treated as some species who suddenly metamorphosised from a prehistoric existence and no one would think of asking them if they wanted war or to stay or evacuate their land or to be part of this country or not". It also remained that giving a mass of people a strip of land for free, in exchange of their land, and expecting peace to reign on the borders was also a *crime*, but for the time being, and with the night of horror fresh on everyone's minds, it looked as if this was where it would be at for the time being.

Tara carried the dinner dishes to the tiny kitchen basin and washed them carefully. The knives whetted, she lay them in place, wiped the table and swept the floor. When she was done, she returned to the baby playing by the hearth. Drawing the baby close, she caressed its head and the baby smiled. Just a few days old, the baby girl was already strong and it seemed she might walk before she crawled. An immense longing seized Tara. Among other things, she wondered what it would be to live in a time when one's fate was not war, like Nakul had always imagined. Thoughts left her dizzy, her heart was heavy with sadness and longing.

Outside, a curtain of rain passed over, and by the time dusk arrived, an explosion of birdsong erupted from the dripping trees. The light began to fade with the chorus of mountain birds returning home, and the reticent sun flickered behind the loosening leave. The length of the night on the sky, which had been full of scales, began to pale at its edge. Dazzling fine as a moth's weightless wing, fell the season's first snow.

Tara kissed the sleeping infant, her tiny breath came deep and regular and warmly sweet, reminding her of Nakul. The baby suddenly opened her eyes. They were startlingly clear and shining with intelligence and curiosity and strength.

Her tiny fingernails dug into Tara's palm—a child of impossible perfection, her fingers uncurled like thin, white leaves, leaving half-smile imprints, and she wondered at the strength in her clear-eyed gaze with strange, gold flecks. Like Amba's. And that pleased her immensely.

It was the end of the old world, but also, a shifting into a new world. As the darkness brightened, her eyes sparkled and tears fell, landing on the baby's cheeks.

"Sleep, little one…there are monsters about and witches who fight."

27

The city hospital doctor was astounded. He was witnessing the sort of stuff he had only read about; but that it was happening in his hospital, what was humanly impossible in medical terms, was surely a miracle! The dead girl had woken up.

Brought to the hospital in the dead of night, exactly a month and seven days ago, by the state Prison Inspection Officer, Nathan Ray, the girl had none of her vital organs functioning after being shot multiple times. The shot, which should have killed her outright but hadn't, was a subject of much conversation. On further scrutiny, the curious-looking green stone inlaid in the girl's amulet was found to be split from the impact of the bullet; its glassy green interior seemed harder than toughened steel, though. Some bullets had drilled clean through her body in several places, missing vital organs, including the heart, and the intestinal wall and the spleen; exiting nearly harmlessly on the opposite side of where they entered. A fraction of a millimetre on either side would have meant certain and painful death. She had lost an immense amount of blood and gone into deep coma. The doctor himself had pronounced her clinically dead, but the stubborn officer had refused to let him pull the plug, and instead, left her in his care after paying all the expenses. And she lay like that, motionless, lifeless, until the doctor made up his mind to appeal to the Medical Board to take the girl off life support; it could be put to better use for someone more needy being his reasoning.

That night, when he was about to leave for home, the nurse came in panting, her face flushed with excitement.

The girl had woken up. Not only was she awake, when he dashed to her room, he found her eating and drinking and looking very calm and composed, as if it was not she who had returned from the brink of death.

Amba had no idea how she came back.

All she knew was that there was nothing at first. Then, she came back; groggy, staggered senses, nerves ablaze, with a sort of humming in her chest, like bees in winter's thaw. The tide of life came in to Amba with all the medusas spinning in its turbulence; thoughts like the tendrils of jellyfish in limbo—like something cut loose, a floating placenta or fallen leaf or a refugee severed from its place of origin.

Memories came back in no particular order. All the things she lived in this birth, mixed with all the eyes she looked into before they died, and all the pain and joy and rage and grief she felt at all times, exploded inside her in a giant burst of light and with one overriding thought.

And the thought was this—

All her life, till now, was murk and depths.

But she was not of the dark waters anymore.

She was of the creatures within.

Why should she be afraid?

She was the source.

THE AFTER

"It's just a dream." That's what he is telling himself. "But, then, why doesn't it end?" Startled by his own voice, Madbull opens his eyes wide and stares confusedly about him. His skin has an achromatic pallidity of such lab creatures, which are kept in long periods of captivity. The waxy face seems too big for the spindly shoulders and legs stunted from lack of sunlight. He rubs his face, trying to get warmth into his icy skin.

"My…skin—Wha-What is happening—c-cannot feel my skin…My tongue…its burning—"

Breathing heavily through a wet mouth, sucking inwards, he darts about in wild, confused arcs. Perhaps he smells those who lurk in desolate darks, peering at him, the mad, malign inhabitant. The walls dissolve into a green, undulating mass, like the rippling flanks of a massive animal, waiting for him; the look in their eyes is dark and insistent.

He hears them coming. His eye sockets expand and his head seems to be trying to turn into a skull. He cowers in a corner. They feel his fear. It is alive and growing. They want to gorge on it. They take the taut wire of his fear and pluck it. His face convulses. From Madbull's throat tears out a long-drawn scream.

WHAT WILL YOU DO WHEN WE COME?